"If I ever get this close to you again,

"I want you to do something," Jackson said.

"What?" Helena asked.

"Slap my face."

Helena's eyes widened, and then a smile formed. "I hardly think it's appropriate for a woman to slap her employer."

"I hardly think it's appropriate for an employer to kiss his cook."

"We were sealing a pact. You were giving me a gift. We were finalizing the deal."

He raised one brow. "Nice of you to let me off the hook."

"It was a nice kiss. I'm not going to slap you if you do it again."

Jackson groaned. "I was afraid of that."

Dear Reader,

Get Caught Reading. It sounds slightly scandalous, romantic and definitely exciting! I love to get lost in a book, and this month we're joining the campaign to encourage reading everywhere. Share your favorite books with your partner, your child, your friends. And be sure to get caught reading yourself!

The popular ROYALLY WED series continues with Valerie Parv's *Code Name: Prince*. King Michael is still missing—but there's a plan to rescue him! In *Quinn's Complete Seduction* Sandra Steffen returns to BACHELOR GULCH, where Crystal finally finds what she's been searching for— and more....

Chance's Joy launches Patricia Thayer's exciting new miniseries, THE TEXAS BROTHERHOOD. In the first story, Chance Randell wants to buy his lovely neighbor's land, but hadn't bargained for a wife and baby! In *McKinley's Miracle*, talented Mary Kate Holder debuts with the story of a rugged Australian rancher who meets his match.

Susan Meier is sure to please with *Marrying Money*, in which a small-town beautician makes a rich man rethink his reasons for refusing love. And Myrna Mackenzie gives us *The Billionaire Is Back*, in which a wealthy playboy fights a strong attraction to his pregnant, single cook!

Come back next month for the triumphant conclusion to ROYALLY WED and more wonderful stories by Patricia Thayer and Myrna Mackenzie. Silhouette Romance always gives you stories that will touch your emotions and carry you away....

Be sure to *Get Caught Reading!*

Mary-Theresa Hussey

Mary-Theresa Hussey
Senior Editor

Please address questions and book requests to:
Silhouette Reader Service
U.S.: 3010 Walden Ave., P.O. Box 1325, Buffalo, NY 14269
Canadian: P.O. Box 609, Fort Erie, Ont. L2A 5X3

The Billionaire Is Back

MYRNA MACKENZIE

SILHOUETTE *Romance*®

Published by Silhouette Books

America's Publisher of Contemporary Romance

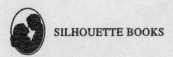

SILHOUETTE BOOKS

ISBN 0-373-19520-6

THE BILLIONAIRE IS BACK

Books by Myrna Mackenzie

Silhouette Desire

The Baby Wish #1046
The Daddy List #1090
Babies and a Blue-Eyed Man #1182
The Secret Groom #1225
The Scandalous Return of Jake Walker #1256
Prince Charming's Return #1361
Simon Says...Marry Me! #1429
At the Billionaire's Bidding #1442
Contractually His #1454
The Billionaire Is Back #1520

*The Wedding Auction

Montana Mavericks

Just Pretending

MYRNA MACKENZIE,

winner of the Holt Medallion honoring outstanding literary talent, has always been fascinated by the belief that within every man is a hero, and inside every woman lives a heroine. She loves to write about ordinary people making extraordinary dreams come true. A former teacher, Myrna lives in the suburbs of Chicago with her husband—who was her high school sweetheart—and her two sons. She believes in love, laughter, music, vacations to the mountains, watching the stars, anything unattached to the words *physical fitness* and letting dust balls gather where they may. Readers can write to Myrna at P.O. Box 225, LaGrange, IL 60525-0225.

HELENA'S RECIPE FOR
HE-WON'T-KNOW-WHAT-HIT-'IM

Mix together
One moonlit, starry night
Your sweetest smile
A dozen heated kisses
A pinch of...him! (optional)

Stir his feelings with a tablespoon of temptation.
Bring him to boil with a smooch at the front porch
and a dreamy "good-night." Send him home to simmer...
until he's ready to say I do!

* * *

**Romance really gets cooking
when Helena's identical twin sister, Lilah,
and her dream man are thrown together
in a dating charade. Don't miss *Blind-Date Bride*
by Myrna Mackenzie, SR #1526,
available June 2001, only from Silhouette Romance.**

Chapter One

"Helena, don't go in there. The man probably has a naked woman in his bedroom. Or maybe more than one."

The sound of raised voices on this quiet stretch of Maine coastland snagged Jackson Castle's attention and he put down his horrendously bad cup of coffee and moved to the open window of the spacious vacation home he'd rented just yesterday. The sight that greeted him had him widening his eyes. A caramel-haired beauty was surrounded by four big males, their arms crossed before them, frowns on their faces. The beauty stood next to her car, smiling patiently, seemingly unaware that she was outnumbered.

"Look, guys, you know and I know that I love you to death, but do I have to tell you for the five millionth time that you're my brothers, not my keepers? And besides, you don't have to worry. I've seen a naked woman before. I've even *been* one from time to time."

"You know darn well what we meant, Helena. The thing is, we just don't want you working for Jackson Castle. Not in such an intimate setting, anyway."

Interesting, Jackson thought with a raised brow, and he realized who the woman must be. This was obviously Helena Austin, his new temporary chef and housekeeper. And her brothers didn't want her working for him?

"I know you don't, Bill," the woman said, a sad, affectionate note in her voice. "And I also know why. You've been listening to all the chatter in town, the rumors that Mr. Castle collects women for a hobby."

One of the other brothers snorted. "Who needs rumors? I saw Castle in town yesterday. I know what he looks like, I know his reputation even without the local rumors, and, well, hell, he's got eight bedrooms here and he's staying alone. What do you think he's planning on using all those beds for?"

The beauty smiled sweetly. "Sleeping, Hank?"

"Sleeping with a lot of different women. Sleeping with *you,* maybe. He wishes," the man standing next to Hank said.

"Thomas, get serious," she drawled, rolling her eyes. "Would you look at me?"

And as the men shifted, Jackson got a good look at her. He sucked in a deep breath.

"She's pregnant," he whispered to himself. And not just pregnant, but wildly pregnant.

"Doesn't matter," Thomas answered.

"Sorry, buddy, but I'm afraid that you couldn't be more wrong," Jackson said under his breath as the woman rolled her eyes in disbelief. If that lady was who he thought she was, it mattered a great deal and perhaps he wouldn't be hiring her after all. This woman was lovely, and lovely was usually a good thing. But pregnant? He happened to have a history with pregnant women. It wasn't a good one, either, beginning with the day his mother had given birth to her unwanted child on a cold, dark, gritty street and ending with his wife conceiving another man's child. And no, he didn't intend on making any more history. At least, not of that nature.

Still, he did have a decided weakness for women in this delicate, vulnerable stage of their lives, and he could see that her brothers' consternation was making them less than heedful of the lady's situation.

She shouldn't be standing in the sun for so long.

He pushed open the door and stepped outside, making his way across the deck and down the stairs to the Austins.

It didn't bother him that he was still looking like the morning after a late night. The details of the project he was planning had kept him awake far into the night, and now his dark hair was still tousled from sleep, his white shirt hung open, he hadn't yet shaved. In short, he looked like the street thug he'd once been rather than the billionaire he'd become. But so much the better. He needed to look a bit formidable right now, and with his height, there was no question that he did.

Jackson cleared his throat.

"Something I can do for you, gentlemen?" he asked, turning dark eyes on the male bodyguards standing before him.

The man standing closest to the beauty frowned and stuck his chest out. "I don't think so. We were just leaving," he said. "All of us. Come on, Helena."

But the lady shook her head. She smiled politely

up at Jackson. She sidestepped her brothers and moved in front of them, and Jackson saw that her eyes were a deep, clear aqua.

"Good morning. You must be Mr. Castle. I hope we didn't wake you. You've probably already guessed that I'm Helena Austin, your new cook and housekeeper, so if you're ready for me, I'll begin." Jackson began to get an idea just why her brothers were getting so protective about her. Her eyes were like open windows, deep and inviting. At close range, that voice, low and sweet, sank right into a man's skin and made him…hot. Jackson forced himself to remember that what she was offering to begin was purely impersonal in nature.

Then she smiled an impish smile and glanced over her shoulder at her brothers. "We don't come as a package," she said. "My brothers are just here on their lunch hour—to wish me well. Aren't you?" she asked.

"Helena," the one called Thomas warned, a groan in his voice, and the lady turned those concerned eyes on her brother.

"Please," she said. "This is my work." The word *work* was so filled with meaning that for a moment, Jackson almost thought she'd meant to say *life*. But, of course, he was just thinking in his own terms. His work had been his life for a long time. He liked it that way.

"Good morning, Ms. Austin," Jackson said, ignoring the glares of the brothers. He supposed they would be happy to know he was on their side. The beauty was definitely enticing, with her voice that could make a man mad with lust and her long caramel-gold hair that summoned images of Lady Godiva riding naked, cloaked only by hair just like Helena's. She was much too enticing for an employee who would be in his home day in and day out. Helena Austin made him think of kissing his way down her bare shoulder, and that just wouldn't fly. He wasn't a man who engaged in real relationships, and a pregnant woman had needs that didn't involve the words *short-term* or *hot*.

"I'm looking forward to working here," the lady said with cheerful determination.

Jackson couldn't help smiling back. He wasn't sure if he would have been able to smile and ignore four golden growling giants if he'd been in her shoes. She was dwarfed by all of them, her condition making her even more fragile looking. But she had an eager, willful expression in her eyes, and the look of a child pretending there are no bogeymen under the bed— when every six-year-old knows that monsters *do* exist.

Jackson had known his share of monsters. He'd battled them into submission, and so he warmed to the lady in spite of himself.

His answering smile must have opened up something within her. "They usually don't bite," she confided. "They're just a little cranky because they were out late playing poker last night. Besides, it's always bothered them that I'm a bit stubborn."

"A bit?" The one named Hank practically roared the words. "Helena, we really need to talk. Hon, maybe you've forgotten that we were going to have lunch together today."

She widened those big aqua eyes in disbelief. "I'll ask Annette to measure your nose tonight to see if it's grown another inch or two, Hank," she promised.

"But I *would* love to have lunch with you. Maybe next week one day?"

His brow furrowed. His eyes clouded over. "This is a mistake, Helena," he said suddenly. "I just don't want to see you jumping before you think again. I don't want to see you make another mistake you'll regret."

Hank's glance fell to her rounded abdomen.

She sucked in a deep breath and raised her chin.

Immediately her brother's face filled with guilt. "I—damn, I'm sorry. I didn't mean that the way it sounded."

She bit down on her lip, then nodded. "I know you didn't."

Admiration seeped into Jackson's soul, as well as a trace of anger at her brothers' actions, and he took a step forward. He didn't know the lady's circumstances, but he knew she had to be feeling more than a bit humiliated in this awkward public situation. This was a conversation that should have taken place elsewhere, and he wondered why it hadn't. As for the rest, well, he might have changed his mind about hiring her, but he darn well wasn't going to dismiss her in front of a crowd, even if that crowd was related to her. This would be done right. In private.

And under the right physical conditions.

Jackson turned his attention to the brothers. "Your sister needs to sit down. It's a shame we can't continue this conversation right now, but I believe Ms. Austin and I have business to conduct. I'd prefer that we do that inside, out of the morning sun," he said, his crisp voice breaking into the silence. He began to button his shirt, first the cuffs and then the rest. He stood taller, in that regal way he had practiced from the day he'd been taken off the streets in this very town and given a chance at life. He assumed the stance that had seen him through success after success. "If you'll excuse us?" he said to her brothers. "Ms. Austin?" He held out his arm.

She shrugged apologetically at her brothers, then placed her slender hand on Jackson's sleeve. The heat of her fingers slipped right through the soft cotton. He had a feeling he understood all too well why her brothers worried. Men would be drawn to this one. They might do many things without thinking.

But he wouldn't.

"We'll talk later," she promised her brothers softly.

"Definitely," Bill promised in return. "No question we'll talk."

Then she turned her back on them and smiled up at Jackson.

Jackson thought that a few more summer flowers might have unfurled at that moment. The light from the lady's smile was that powerful.

Still, he kept walking. He led her up the steps of the deck, across the wooden planking. He opened the door and showed her inside the large blue-and-white kitchen that filled the back of the house.

"Please, have a seat," he said, gesturing to a chair.

"Of course." She glanced around the room as she sat, her gaze taking in the polished surface of his island cooktop, the inlaid wood of the built-in refrigerator. "I'm sorry about what happened outside."

"No problem at all."

"My brothers have always been a bit overprotective, but lately they've gone overboard."

"They care for you."

She raised her brows. "They do, but they don't have any real reason to worry. I'm just here, as you know, to cook."

She stared at him intently, and he figured she was worrying that he might have overheard what he had, in fact, overheard. That he might have wondered if this conversation was going to take on personal undertones.

He glanced at the pathetic pot of sludgy coffee he'd made. "I definitely need a cook," he said, half to himself.

Her laughter bubbled up as her gaze followed his. "Well, you've certainly got all the equipment to produce some masterful meals, Mr. Castle." She jumped up, ruining all of Jackson's well-intentioned efforts to get her off her feet. She circled the kitchen, eyeing it with what almost seemed a lustful intent as she brushed her fingertips over the polished surface of his island cooktop, as she breathed in the scent of the wood cabinets and raked her palm across the top-of-the-line refrigerator.

A hint of a sigh escaped her. "It's beautiful, you know. This place, it's a cook's dream come true, Mr. Castle. I'm not sure you can really relate, but to me, your kitchen is a bit like fantasyland. All this golden wood and glass. You've got some absolutely wonderful appliances." She gazed up at him, a dreamy look on her face.

He almost grinned at her choice of words, even though he was sure she was referring to the world-class espresso machine she had glanced toward. Still, the word *fantasy* was oddly appropriate for the moment, because watching her speak, it occurred to Jackson that Helena Austin's lips were like pink candy, and would tempt any man to cover her mouth with his own and gorge on the honey that lay within.

Jackson took a deep breath and reminded himself that this was business and Helena Austin's lips were forbidden fruit. He didn't hire women he desired. The possibilities for difficulties were just too great. Hiring a woman he desired who was also *pregnant* could only serve as a reminder of the times in his life he preferred not to dwell on. Still, he'd had years of working with employees. Telling this lady she wouldn't suit wasn't simply a case of sending her out the door. It was a delicate matter, especially since she was already coveting his appliances.

"I'm glad you approve," he said, keeping his tone carefully light.

She tilted her head in acknowledgment of his comment. "I do, and I'm sorry you're having to scramble to find someone to put your lovely kitchen to use. Abe Howard at the employment agency told me that you'd unexpectedly found yourself without a cook. That must be incredibly disconcerting," the tawny-haired beauty said. That there might be a problem beyond the fact that he was temporarily without a cook obviously hadn't occurred to her. For half a second the sympathy in her eyes and her concerned tone touched something within him, and he regretted having to turn her down when she clearly wanted to work here.

Then Jackson's gaze dipped low on her body. She might be sinfully pretty with an endearing manner, but she was still just as tempting—and pregnant—as she'd been two minutes ago.

"Ms. Austin," he began.

"*Helena,*" she said. "I'm sorry. I should have

thought. It's still early. Maybe you haven't even had breakfast yet. If not, don't worry. I'll just slip into an apron and get started.''

Jackson raised one brow and gazed at the woman's lips as she finished up her pretty little speech. He was a man who prided himself on maintaining a cool head under all circumstances, but he couldn't help wondering just how the words *slip into an apron* could sound so incredibly erotic. Must be the fact that it *was* still early morning, and he had only thrown off the covers and tugged on his pants less than thirty minutes ago. And here he had a beautiful woman offering, in a low, stroking voice that clearly belonged behind closed bedroom doors, to slip into an apron and cook him breakfast. His thoughts filtered in from some secret hiding place, bringing a frown to Jackson's face. Helena Austin's voice or what she wore was none of his affair, and besides, the lady wasn't staying, anyway. He obviously hadn't been specific enough when he'd been outlining his needs to Abe.

''I appreciate you getting over here so quickly, Helena,'' he said, automatically falling into the commanding tone of voice that had led him off the backstreets of St. Louis and down the path of success. ''But while it's true that I've found myself unexpectedly in need of a cook, I suppose I should have told Abe that there might be certain limitations on this position. You—forgive me, but you appear to be pregnant.''

She raised one brow and smiled. ''You appear to be very astute, Mr. Castle.''

He couldn't help returning the smile. The woman wasn't just pregnant. She was round and full and darn near close to time, he'd bet. A man would have had to be facing in the opposite direction not to have noticed.

"All right, then, you're *very* pregnant, Helena."

"I take it that's a problem?"

It was more than a problem.

Still, he'd been employing people for many years now. He knew the laws regarding hiring practices. Besides, even if there hadn't been a law, a man didn't just turn a competent employee away on a personal whim, even if that personal roadblock was made of solid granite.

Unless that employee was going to be bringing him breakfast in bed.

Jackson promised himself he'd be tactful and gentle when he broke the bad news.

At the same moment, Helena leaned forward slightly, waiting for him to tell her if he had a problem with her, and he caught a faint whiff of her lemony scent. He had a sudden vision of her applying perfume, her fingers sliding over the pulse point at her throat, stroking behind the delicate bend of her knee, dipping low between her breasts. He also had a sudden vision of himself jumping off a building he'd jumped off before. The jumping was fine. It was the landing on the unforgiving ground that had been a problem.

Jackson forced himself to stop thinking about how Helena Austin smelled. Something was definitely wrong with his libido this morning. He might be a healthy male, but he certainly didn't go around mentally undressing his employees. It just wasn't right.

"Mr. Castle?" she said, and he read the uncertainty in her eyes. "*Is* there a problem?"

Think fast, Castle, he ordered himself, but what he

noticed was that there was no ring on her left hand.
No obvious social impediments. Only the very real
ones from his past, the knowledge that a man with
emotional limits had no business getting too close to
a vulnerable woman. Jackson couldn't think of a
woman much more vulnerable than one having a baby
on her own. Damn.

Think faster, Castle. He cleared his throat.

"I'll be doing a fair amount of entertaining while
I'm in Sloane's Cove," he told her. "I brought my
regular cook and sometime housekeeper with me.
Henry is a big man. He's capable of lifting heavy
trays, moving furniture and working for hours standing when it's necessary. Unfortunately, he broke his
arm rock climbing yesterday, and he had to be sent
home to Boston."

"Yes, I know," she said. "I hope he's all right.
He'll cook again?"

"Of course," he said, smiling at her priorities.
"Abe told you about Henry, then?"

She shook her head. "I heard courtesy of the town
grapevine."

When he raised one brow, she shrugged. "Sloane's
Cove may be a Maine tourist town, we may cater to
wealthy travelers, but we're still a small town at heart.
News zips around quickly. We don't have many secrets."

That was too bad, Jackson thought, since he had a
secret he didn't want to let out of the bag. At least,
not just yet.

"At any rate, what I'm trying to say, Helena, is
that I'm really looking for someone who is physically
capable of a great deal of wear and tear." It was true
enough, even if it wasn't the real reason for his re-

luctance. A man just didn't tell a potential employee that he found her too tempting.

She tilted her head, a look of pure sympathy in those big aqua eyes. Then she shook her head.

"Do not underestimate me, Mr. Castle. I'm capable of many things you would not believe. But more important, I have to tell you with all honesty that you don't have a lot of options here. This is coastal Maine in late June. The tourist season is already beginning. A good employee is all but impossible to find. A good cook is even more difficult to obtain."

Whether she realized it or not, her hand had crept over her abdomen as if shielding her child from his rejection. Jackson felt a thread of guilt. He'd been a child the last time he'd had to worry about money or finding his next meal, but he hadn't forgotten one moment of the fear.

"I'll make sure Abe finds work for you," he offered gently.

"I don't exactly need the work," she said just as gently.

"Well, then—"

"Then why am I here?" she asked, finishing his question, her blue-green eyes filled with humor. He wondered how those eyes would look if a man coaxed her into his bed and gave her pleasure.

Not that he'd ever know.

Jackson fought to concentrate on the topic at hand.

"Why are you here?" he agreed, and found that his voice had drifted low and deep.

She blinked and sucked in a breath.

"I'm, well, what can I say?" She held out her hands, palms up. "Abe is an old friend. He needed someone for you, and I've just finished a job, so I was available when he finally connected with me this morning. Besides, he knew that I had a thing for your kitchen.''

Jackson shook his head and grinned. ''Oh yes, my appliances. You have a…thing for my kitchen.''

She nodded briskly. ''I worked here three years ago when the Hamiltons owned the house and were re-modeling it. They let me help them design their dream kitchen. Unfortunately, Mrs. Hamilton died that winter. It's been closed up since then. This is the first summer Mr. Hamilton has opted to rent it out.''

''So you want me for my kitchen? My trash compactor? My refrigerator?''

''Mmm, and that incredible blender,'' she agreed, ''but mostly I want you for the experience. I don't really need the money. My husband's life insurance was enough for me to live comfortably after he died, but I've been making up recipes and writing cook-books since I could first reach the stovetop. It's more than a living. It's my passion, and it helps tremen-dously to have an audience to try my recipes out on. Abe told me that you'd be entertaining a great deal, which is somewhat unusual around here even for the rich. Most people are here to get away from the stress of business and entertaining, so, yes, you'll do fabu-lously, especially since my work in progress focuses on party fare.''

Jackson fought not to smile. ''I'll do, will I?''

''Fabulously,'' she repeated.

He breathed out a sigh. ''Any other reason why I should hire you?''

She looked at him with big innocent eyes. ''Yes, of course.''

''Care to be more specific?.''

She shrugged, lifting one delicate shoulder. "Well, I *am* very good."

He hoped she was talking about cooking. There was no way he would allow himself to imagine she meant anything else. He refused to let his body react the way it wanted to.

"And I donate twenty percent of all the profits on my books to the Sloane's Cove Children's Clinic. Helping me finish this book more quickly would be the charitable thing to do."

"What makes you think I'm in any way charitable?" No one knew what he had come here to do. He was certain of that. He wanted to make sure things stayed that way.

She looked slightly disappointed. "I know you're a very busy man, Mr. Castle, but don't you even have time to watch yourself on television? You were featured on *The World's Most Wealthy Bachelors* about a month ago. The commentator mentioned your pet charities. There were a number of them."

Jackson's blood went suddenly cool. *"The World's Most Wealthy Bachelors…"* He seemed to remember his assistant mentioning that his face had been splashed across the nation's TV screens, but he'd been in the middle of a meeting with one of his most loyal clients. He'd been locating toys and baubles and interesting bits of art for the wealthy for years. His business had made him rich, and this client had been one of his first. The television program hadn't seemed important.

It was important now, but only because the lovely Ms. Austin was blushing a dusky rose that did enticing things to the creamy skin that covered her cheeks, her slender throat and the V that dipped beneath the pale blue fabric of her dress. She was a pregnant woman, and she was alone at a time in her life when no woman probably wanted to be alone. A woman carrying another man's baby. A disconcerting vision of his ex-wife and his ex-coworker rose up. He shut it down.

"You say 'wealthy bachelor' as if I've come here expressly to find one for myself, Mr. Castle," she said suddenly. "I assure you that you couldn't be more wrong. I don't mean to be rude, but truthfully, I'm not interested in you or any other bachelor. I've had one husband and I don't want another. All I want to do is cook and fulfill my duties as housekeeper. If you hire me, I can promise you that I'll offer you a taste of my best cooking and nothing else. You won't have to worry about me giving you longing looks unless you're dangling a new recipe just out of reach."

And just like that she made him feel like ten kinds of a heel. The woman didn't need a job, and yes, he'd had the sneaking suspicion when Henry had gotten hurt that he would have trouble finding a replacement. Abe had said that she had an impeccable résumé and that he could supply many references.

He, Jackson Castle, was the one who was desperate, not this woman standing so bravely before him. He knew darn well that his size, his height and his dark hair and eyes had made men quake before. Yet here he stood glaring at a woman who had cheerfully offered to help him out of a fix.

Jackson tried out a reassuring smile. "You think I'm in desperate straits, then?"

"Only if you want to eat."

"I generally do that several times a day."

"And if you want to feed your guests."

"Guests tend to get testy if you ask them over for hours and only serve them water."

"Understandable. My pregnancy won't be a problem, Mr. Castle," she assured him. "I know how to talk people into helping me when I need it. I won't jeopardize my baby's health. I promise you won't have a lawsuit on your hands, if that's your concern."

"It's not, and I apologize if I gave that impression. I'll have to thank Abe for sending you my way."

"You're okay with me, then?"

"I'm ecstatic, Helena," he said.

"You lie well, Mr. Castle, but that's okay." Jackson would have sworn that the words *I've been lied to before* hung in the air between them, and her hand curved gently over her abdomen again. Protecting. He wanted to drive that tension from her eyes.

"Welcome to my home, then," he said, holding out his hand. "I'll be in town for about three weeks. Will that be okay?" Did she have three weeks before her baby arrived?

She smiled and took his hand, her small, smooth palm lying against his skin.

"I'll be fine. I'll make a real effort not to give birth midparty, and I'll do my best to please your guests, Mr. Castle," she said. "You're in for a few surprises."

He hoped not. The surprise of Helena herself was more than enough to deal with right now. Already he was remembering the feel of her hand in his own. He was wanting to touch her again.

It was going to be hell trying to hide the attraction he felt for her.

The lady had been clear. He doubted that she would welcome him touching her on a regular basis. It wasn't in her job description.

But it was definitely in his mind.

Chapter Two

"I finally saw that Jackson Castle you're working for. Good shoulders. Good chest. Good everything. He's going to make your life hell, Helena."

Helena glanced up from her market basket to look into Alma Frost's eyes. Alma was a friend who owned the local fruit market, and she had wandered outside to the open-air bins to track Helena down.

Helena tried out a smile. "You're delusional, Alma. I'm not interested in Jackson Castle's chest."

"Then you must have died and not told me. Just because you're pregnant doesn't mean that you've stopped being a woman. He's a man made for making love."

Helena shrugged, shooting for a disinterested attitude. "All right, he's handsome. I'll give you that." Might as well. It had been silly to try to fool Alma. The woman was no slouch. She could zero in on a person's feelings without even trying. But Helena wasn't too sure she wanted to examine her feelings about Jackson Castle too closely herself, much less let anyone else start dissecting them. The man *was* just shockingly handsome, and there was something incredibly sensual about the way he looked at a person. Staring up into those silver-gray eyes of his this morning, Helena had felt as if she were losing herself in his gaze. Beneath those long dark lashes he'd studied her as if he knew that she was wearing a lace chemise beneath her dress and that she had a beauty mark on the upper curve of her right breast. It was definitely best to maintain a distance from a man such as that. To be cool even if the very thought of Jackson was making her rather warm.

"Kind of hard to believe a man who looks so pleasing could be turning up so much trouble in town this afternoon."

That got Helena's attention. She stopped gathering fruit and turned to stare at Alma. "What are you talking about?"

It was Alma's turn to shrug. "You've probably heard that he's having a big gathering here in the park in three weeks. Some totally huge hoopla in honor of the late Oliver Davis, who used to shoot through here now and then twenty years ago. Apparently this Oliver knew a lot of people who want to be a part of the hoopla. The town and all the towns on Mount Desert Island and the neighboring mainland are being besieged by rich people suddenly trying to get rooms."

"People are always trying to get rooms here in the summer."

"Not like this. It's like it's suddenly raining billionaires and some of them are being none too nice, I've heard. But that's not all. Your Mr. Castle isn't just planning the town's biggest wienie roast ever.

He's been roaming around, asking all kinds of questions today. And I don't mean questions about how much a quart of blueberries costs. Personal stuff. Details about all of us who live here. That's just a little too unusual for an outsider.''

Helena placed another apple in her half-full basket. She knew what Alma meant. Already three other people had asked her about Jackson. It wasn't that curiosity was a sin, but the wealthy people who vacationed in Sloane's Cove generally didn't even notice the locals. If they did notice, their attitude seemed to be that the people were just part of the vacation scenery, like the seagulls, the rocky shoreline or the waves lapping against the pier.

"Maybe he's writing a book or he's trying to drum up some press for his party and he wants to highlight the locals?" Helena offered.

"You think?" Alma seemed interested. She fluffed up her hair.

Helena couldn't help smiling. "You want me to corner him and demand that he tell me his secrets?"

"Maybe. If you make him get naked first and let me watch."

"Alma…" Helena drawled.

"Oh, all right. I'm just wondering is all. Why is he asking all those questions outsiders don't usually ask? He's not the kind we see through here too often."

"Maybe he's just naturally curious." But Helena didn't really think so. In spite of the fact that he'd been kind to her, there was a distance to him. He struck her as a man who kept to himself and liked other people to do the same. She didn't actually know that to be the truth. In fact, her brothers were right when they'd said she didn't know much about the man and that not knowing much about men had gotten her in trouble before. It had. Many times, ending with her marriage.

After choosing the wrong kind of man too many times, she'd given up romance and married for friendship against the wishes of her family. Since neither she nor Peter expected love, she'd thought she was being smart. The idea had been for her to gain experience cooking and at the same time help her husband with his business. Her dinner parties had brought in clients…right until the day she'd discovered that he'd fallen in love with someone else. She should have let go, let him at least be happy, but she'd hung on, she'd gotten pregnant. Two months later Peter had died in a boating accident, and now it was too late to make things right.

So, yes, she really should stop jumping into things with both feet, and she'd be wise to curb her own natural curiosity about Jackson. She wasn't even going to allow herself to wonder why she found the slash of his mouth so fascinating.

"Helena?" Alma waved her hand in front of her face.

Helena jerked away from her thoughts, nearly spilling the apples from her basket. She aimed a hasty smile at her friend. "I'm sure Jackson's just asking questions because that's how he runs his business, Alma," she said, composing herself.

Alma didn't reply. In fact, her eyes had taken on a slightly worried look. She held up her hand as if to stop Helena, but Helena shook her head.

"Don't believe me, but I'm sure that's it," Helena continued. "After all, he's made a fortune supplying the rich and famous with baubles and toys and decorations for their mansions, and we have plenty of expert craftsmen here. He probably asks a lot of questions wherever he goes. How else would he find all those hidden treasures? He might even be planning on scoping out the local talent while he's here getting ready for his celebration. I don't really know, but if you're that curious, I could ask Jackson.''

''Ask Jackson what?''

The deep male voice startled her, and Helena whirled. She teetered as she came up against the hard planes of Jackson's chest.

He grasped her arms to steady her, and she nearly gasped at the feel of his fingers against her skin. Time seemed to freeze. Her voice ceased to function. For four mad seconds she wanted to stay there, to ask him to keep touching her. She wanted to burrow closer into those strong, protective arms.

Oh no, tell me I didn't really think that, and please don't let the man be able to read minds. After that program on television, Jackson probably had women bumping into him every day, women who wanted to be the next Mrs. Castle. That wasn't her. She had never, ever been the type to want someone to protect her. On the contrary, she was the one who always did the leading, the charging ahead, the protecting.

''Excuse me. I'm so sorry,'' she finally managed to say, taking a deep breath.

''Don't be sorry, but really, you shouldn't be carrying so much. Let me,'' he admonished, letting go with one hand to take the basket she held in her arms.

Helena tried to take it back. ''Oh no, I work for you. That means I carry things, so you don't need to do that. Besides, it's a very light basket. Only a few packages. An ant could carry it.''

He stared down at her. ''But you're a woman. A pregnant woman. Humor me,'' he ordered in that low, sexy whisper. And because his voice triggered thoughts of him whispering over her in the dark confines of a bed, Helena clamped her mouth closed and humored him.

''What did you want to ask me?'' His low voice vibrated through Helena's body where his palm still connected with her skin. A slight shiver of something feminine and foolish darted through her, and Helena took a deep breath.

As if realizing that he held her prisoner, Jackson let go. He looked down at her, an apology in his eyes.

''Alma is curious about your intentions here in Sloane's Cove,'' she told him.

Jackson stared down into Helena's eyes. ''My... intentions?''

She nodded slowly, marveling at how she had to tip her head back to retain direct contact with that mesmerizing gaze. She forced herself to take another deep breath.

''Yes, you're a wealthy man. You frolic with the rich and famous. It seems unlikely that you'd be interested in the lives of those of us who reside in small-town America, but—''

He was studying her closely now, his silver-eyed gaze still very direct and intense, as if she were relating words of the utmost importance to him.

''Yes?'' he asked in that silky voice.

Helena cleared her throat. In spite of the heat that climbed her body, she didn't back away. ''You seem awfully curious about what makes Sloane's Cove tick.''

Jackson raised one brow. "There've been complaints?"

"Of course not. People are flattered that you're talking to them. They're just astounded that a man of your station would care to know about their daily lives. To a man who vacations in exotic places with exotic...people—'' okay, she'd almost said *women* ''—we're very plain vanilla, I would think.''

A slow smile lifted those gorgeous and no doubt talented lips. "There's nothing wrong with vanilla, Helena.''

"But vanilla isn't very exciting,'' she insisted.

He grinned. "You've been watching too much television. You think I'm so shallow that I'm only looking for excitement?"

She thought he was dangerous and incredibly complex. When his gaze dropped to her lips for two seconds, she thought she just might faint.

"So, you're not here looking for excitement?'' she managed to say.

He shook his head slowly. "I'm here for several reasons, but excitement's not one of them. Six months ago I lost an old friend who used to summer here now and then. Oliver Davis was a humanitarian. Sloane's Cove is where we met. It seemed appropriate to have a celebration of his life in the place where he first came alive for me.''

His voice grew warmer when he spoke of his friend. He gazed into Helena's eyes as if the memories of his past were written there.

"He must have been a great man,'' Alma said suddenly, causing Helena to jump slightly. She'd almost forgotten that she and Jackson were standing in a public place and that Alma was a part of the conversation.

When Jackson took a long, deep breath, straightened his shoulders and took a step backward, Helena thought that he might have forgotten, too.

"He was that," Jackson agreed, turning to look at Alma, who was holding out her hand. He smiled and gave her a handshake, studying her name tag. "Ms. Frost? Would you be the legendary and fascinating woman who's won the jelly competition at the local fair for the last three summers?"

Alma laughed out loud. "Mr. Castle, I don't care what anyone says. You're good people in my book. But actually, I owe my success to Helena. She taught me everything I know, and she lets me win by not entering the contests. Helena has a way of taking on pet causes and helping people out when they need it. I'm just one of the lucky ones she's aided."

Jackson turned his attention to Helena. He studied her carefully with those silvery eyes until she thought that her skin would turn pink. "Abe must have kept some secrets from me. I find that very interesting," he said.

"Not as interesting as what's coming down the street," Alma answered. "Helena's brothers don't appear to have missed the fact that you had your hands on her in broad daylight just a second ago." She nodded toward the end of the street where the Austin brothers were headed their way looking less than pleased.

Helena groaned. She grabbed Jackson's hand. "Come on."

He stood his ground. "If your brothers want to talk to me, then we'll talk."

She stared up at him, frustration filling her soul. "I don't feel comfortable with that. Yesterday they were being polite, but then, you and I hadn't had any physical contact. Today we have, sort of, and they're a little edgy. They don't know that you were just trying to keep me from falling. At the moment my brothers are very much into the business of acting first and asking questions later. I surprised them by taking this job suddenly, and since my husband died, they seem to spend an inordinate amount of time worrying about me."

"Good. They should. And I'm not going to disappear every time they show up."

Helena peered around Jackson's massive frame. She could see Hank barreling down the street, heat practically vibrating off his body, his chin urging the world to "take a swing." Her other brothers were not far behind.

She turned plaintive eyes up to Jackson. He was looking every bit as resolute as her brothers. Like a mountain, she was pretty sure that he would be tough to move. She was also pretty sure that Jackson had used his fists before. He had that look. No way did she want anyone fighting about her. Didn't she already have enough guilt left over from her marriage?

"Jackson?" she asked. "Could you take me out of here now? I'm pretty sure that conflict is not good for the baby," she said solemnly.

He swore beneath his breath.

She refrained from saying that swearing was probably not something the baby should hear, either.

"Name the place," he told her.

"In here." She motioned toward a small bookstore three doors down. "It's my sister's store."

"Your brothers won't follow you in there?"

"They won't fight in front of Lilah. She's the good sister," Helena explained. "The delicate one."

He leaned back, one brow raised in a question. "The good one?"

"It's a relative term," she explained, pulling him toward the store.

"Of course," he agreed, a trace of laughter in his voice. "This sister of yours, would she be the one who looks almost just like you?" Jackson said as Lilah opened the door and motioned them inside.

Helena glanced back over her shoulder. "Most people would say we look exactly alike. We're twins."

He shook his head. "I see that, but I don't buy into that 'exactly alike' part. There are definite differences, and it's more than just the fact that your eyes are a slightly different shade of blue."

Her eyes widened. Most people didn't even notice the differences, they were so busy keying in on the similarities. But her sister was waiting. Helena stepped inside.

Lilah closed the door behind her and leaned on it. "Hello, love. Mr. Castle," she said, holding out her hand. "It seems you've already met the rest of my family." She smiled broadly as her brothers drew up in front of her store and halted. "They'll come in in a minute," she confided. "When they've cooled down. It's an unwritten law we settled on years ago to protect my standing in the business community. I'd heard you'd kind of shaken up the Austin clan."

"Lilah, the man hasn't done anything." Helena crossed her arms and paced back and forth. "Can you believe them?"

Lilah eyed Jackson up and down. A slow smile lifted her lips. She motioned her sister over to the side and put her lips to Helena's ear.

"He looks like a man who knows a lot about sex."

Helena felt her cheeks growing warm. She fanned herself slightly with a book she took off a shelf.

Lilah grinned more broadly.

"It's hot in here," Helena said by way of explanation.

It wasn't, and Lilah obviously knew it, but true to the first rule of sisterhood, she didn't say so.

"I'm pleased to meet you, Ms. Austin," Jackson said suddenly, turning to Lilah and putting down Helena's basket. "You won't mind looking after Helena for a minute, will you? Don't let her pick up anything too heavy."

"Of course not," Lilah agreed.

"Where are you going?" Helena asked.

"To talk to your brothers, of course."

"That might be dangerous."

Jackson's smile was slow and lazy. Helena had a feeling that he'd known more than his share of danger.

"You won't hurt them, will you?"

"I try never to beat on the family members of my employees," he said, pulling open the door and stepping outside and down the walk right into the center of her brothers.

Through the thick glass of the bookstore window Helena could just make out some of what he was saying.

"I applaud your concern, but for Helena's sake, I suggest you accept the fact that your sister has chosen to work for me," he said. "As her employer, I can assure you that I'll see to her welfare. That means I will catch her if she looks as if she's going to fall, I will help her to a chair if I think she's been on her feet too long, I will not allow her to carry anything that weighs too much, and I will not allow anyone, including her brothers, to cause her and the baby undue stress.''

To Helena's surprise, her brothers shut up for the duration of the speech.

Silence reigned for several seconds, then they formed a huddle. Some arguing ensued, then more quiet chatter.

Finally they broke ranks.

"We'll agree to your terms, for now," Frank said. "Mostly because we know Helena feels so strongly about her career."

"But we'll be close by," Thomas added.

"You should know that she's not like those women you know in Paris." Helena leaned forward at Bill's words. She wondered how many women Jackson had in Paris. He certainly wasn't refuting Bill's words.

"And she's probably getting married soon," Hank concluded.

Jackson didn't bat an eye in spite of what she'd told him earlier. He simply nodded.

Helena turned with shock to her sister.

"I meant to tell you," Lilah whispered. "The boys were in earlier. They think you've had enough time to mourn Peter, considering the circumstances. They told me that since Thomas got married, we're the only two single Austins and they want to see us settled. You first. The pregnancy thing, you know."

Helena stiffened. "I'm not getting married again, Lilah.''

"Tell that to the boys. They were already naming names of potential mates. Keith Garlan. Bob Mason. All very nice men, as they put it."

Groaning, Helena clutched Lilah's arm. "I am especially not getting married to those so-called 'good' men our brothers will choose. I'm sure the boys have drawn up a list of what they see as my virtues and are marketing me as the cure-all for whatever ails a good man. But I've had enough of men who see me as a solution to their problems and then don't know what to do with me once their problems are solved. Our brothers are going to be disappointed in me, I'm afraid."

"I told them so, love, but you know how that goes."

She did. "Thanks for sticking up for me, anyway."

Turning toward Lilah, Helena gave her a smile. Lilah countered with a hug. "You've always been the one to stick up for everyone else, sweetie, to solve the world's problems. It's your turn for the rest of us to watch over you. I suppose in my own way I'm as bad as the boys."

They both turned to stare at the mulish looks on their brothers' faces.

Helena giggled. "I doubt that very much. Just so you know, if they turn their attention to finding you a husband, I'll help you evade them."

"Just like when we were kids," Lilah said, her voice going soft. "Everyone should have a sister like you. Or even brothers like ours. At least we know they love us."

That was true, Helena thought, watching the handsome determined face of Jackson as he gestured to her brothers. She remembered from the show on television that he had no siblings. No family at all. He was alone.

Almost alone, she thought, giving Lilah a quick hug and a word of thanks before stepping out the door. Jackson had gone outside to help her, but she had never been the helpless sort.

Her unnerving physical reaction to the man was what had really sent her scurrying inside to collect her thoughts and tame her impulses. Because her brothers were partly right. Jackson was a danger.

But not because he coveted her body the way her brothers thought he did.

The real reason was that *she* was attracted to *him*. He was simply and undeniably a woman beacon. One look at that hard jawline and she wanted to lean close. To close her mouth over his skin, to taste his essence. And that was just plain wrong and stupid for a woman with her past.

But at least now she'd admitted the truth. Now it should be a simple task to make those feelings go away.

"Let's go home," she said quietly. "You must be hungry."

Bad choice of words. For two seconds his eyes turned fierce and powerful. For two seconds she realized that he was going to be a terribly difficult man to ignore. For two seconds more, she thought her brothers were going to start swearing.

"She's safe," Jackson promised her brothers. "But for the next three weeks she's mine. Understood?"

And something distinctly male passed between them, because her brothers did not attack Jackson.

"You'll protect her," Thomas suggested.

"Absolutely," Jackson agreed.

"And you'll understand if we still act as her brothers," Hank added.

"A woman in Helena's condition needs to be treated right," Jackson said.

"We're not going to disappear," Frank warned.

"She'll want her family close by," Jackson conceded.

"And we meant that part about the marriage," Bill added.

Jackson stood silent a second. "I'm not in the market for a wife, if that's what you're implying, but I definitely don't require my employees to be single," he said quietly.

Helena felt a strong urge to throw a tantrum, something she hadn't done since she was three years old. Instead she pushed forward into the midst of all those males.

"Excuse me, but despite your assumptions, I really am a grown woman. I can take care of myself," she said.

But neither her brothers or Jackson answered her. They simply exchanged "the look," the one that guys seem to understand. And then they parted ways.

Her brothers still looked restive.

Jackson still looked immovable.

"I don't like this one bit," she said as Jackson took her by the hand.

But the truth was that the feel of his fingertips against her palm was unbearably seductive. She liked it too much.

There were two things on his mind right now, Jackson thought later that day as he sat in the dining room and watched Helena moving around the kitchen in her pretty yellow dress.

The first was that he'd gotten word from his office that Barrett Richards, his chief competitor, the man who'd seduced and impregnated Jackson's wife, had heard the news about Oliver's celebration and was planning to pay a visit to the Cove, ostensibly to attend the party. That he could deal with. Anger for Barrett Richards might once have consumed him, but the man was nothing but an annoyance now.

What concerned Jackson more was the niggling idea that was forming in his mind, and that idea was tangled up with his new cook. Just as the sunlight was tangling in her hair, turning it soft and golden.

The fanciful thought bothered him. He didn't want to notice the details of Helena's appearance. Not the way her long neck curved so delicately into her shoulder, not the way her apron snugged in just beneath her breasts in a tantalizing fashion, not the way she splayed her hand now and then across the place where her child rested. He didn't want to spend too much time in the lady's presence if he could help it.

He recalled the warmth her friend and her family had demonstrated for her today, the loyalty that she'd inspired, the physical beauty of the woman, and he knew Helena Austin spoke to places in him that were rusty and unworkable and best left unexamined. He'd learned at a young age that strong emotions were to be avoided at all costs. He'd held to that theory in spite of everything. Now, after decades of practice, he no longer had the ability to even feel with any real depth, it seemed. His wife had told him so repeatedly.

Still, Helena made him feel restless and urgent, and that was unacceptable. He probably should have found her another place to work. He wished he wasn't thinking about asking for her help, tying himself to her in still more complicated ways.

But his experience in town had taught him something today. He was going about things all wrong here, creating suspicion where he wanted to inspire trust. Because this wasn't his usual business. This was outside his realm of expertise, and he was a man who'd grown used to calling on experts when he needed help. He needed help now.

He had come to Sloane's Cove for a reason he couldn't simply ignore. To finally say goodbye to a man who had been unbelievably kind to him, and to do it in a meaningful way. The plans for the celebration were public knowledge, but there was more. Nothing that could be divulged, unfortunately, even though the rest of the plan was relatively simple. Just a few acts of benevolence conducted in Oliver's name. Just a bit of secrecy and some minor detective work to decide whom those acts of benevolence should benefit.

But how to decide who was the neediest, who was the most worthy?

Good question. Successful as he was, he was floundering right now. He'd already aroused suspicions today while trying to obtain information. And raising suspicions would muddy the waters, make it impossible to do this one good thing.

Like it or not, he needed an accomplice, someone who already knew and understood the people of the town.

And he knew who he wanted. She was here, beautiful and sunny and singing in his kitchen.

Helena. A lifelong local, a woman with a heart, who took on pet causes.

He had a pet cause. He needed such a woman, even if this particular woman made his palms sweat and his body ache in unforgivable ways.

Jackson took a deep breath as he finally allowed the thought to form, as he watched Helena through the open doorway while he pretended to push papers around on the dining-room table. He tried to back away from this decision. Getting close to Helena was risky. She reminded him too much of things in which he no longer believed. And she belonged to this place where his memories were all jumbled and wild, sweet and yet too painful to examine. He should maintain a strict professional distance.

But still…

He needed Helena. He wanted her. He rose and walked into the kitchen.

Helena stopped singing at the sound of his entrance. She turned, the smile still on her lovely pink lips. A smile that made him want to move closer when that would be a terrible mistake.

Jackson felt like groaning with frustration.

Instead he couldn't help smiling in response to her expression.

"You…wanted me for something?" she asked.

Did he want her for something? He did, but she wouldn't want to know *all* the things he wanted her for but would never allow himself. He fought to find his voice, to keep it light and crisp.

"There's something I'd like to talk to you about," he agreed. "I hear that walking is often prescribed for…women in your condition."

Helena grinned. "Ah yes, my condition."

He tilted his head. "Do you walk?"

"I do many things," she agreed with a smile. "Walking is just one of my many talents."

"Let's walk, then," he said, holding out his hand. "And I'll tell you what I want."

Chapter Three

"I assume we're talking about food? You want to discuss your preferences, the way you want things done?" Helena tried to sound professional, but the intensity in Jackson's eyes was making her imagine all kinds of things. Fantasy things. Foolish, improbable things. Heavens, she was worse than her brothers, imagining that Jackson had actually looked at her with hunger in his eyes.

She placed her hands on her stomach to remind herself that she wasn't going to be attracting men in that way for a while.

Jackson shook his head as he led her down the stairs, headed for the small paved path that divided the rocky shore from the beach. "You'd ask that of a man who downed three of those macadamia brownies you made? I'm an astute businessman, Helena. When I find someone who knows their business, I don't interfere with the way they do things."

"Then—?"

Jackson stopped at the bottom of the steps and turned to face Helena. The ocean was at his back, the wind lifted his dark hair. His eyes were on a level with her own.

"How well do you know the people of this town, Helena?" he asked.

"I've lived here all my life."

"And you feel an affection for your neighbors?"

She smiled. "I think it goes deeper than affection. When you share a history, a way of life and a town, there's a special kind of bond."

He nodded as if digesting a bit of news he hadn't been privy to before. She wondered if he'd ever known that kind of closeness.

"So if good fortune befell a few of the people of this town, you'd be happy?" he asked.

"Of course, but I don't understand."

He touched two fingers to her lips. "There are people...sometimes there are people who are more deserving and in need of good fortune than others. You know a few of those."

"I suppose I do," she whispered against his fingertips, trying to stop the shiver of awareness from passing through her to him.

His lids closed slightly, as if she'd failed in her attempt.

Jackson swallowed visibly. He slid his fingers away from her mouth. "And if someone told you that there was a possibility that some of those people could be helped, you'd want to see that happen?"

"I'd want that very much. You're thinking of playing Santa Claus?"

Jackson smiled slightly. "I wouldn't quite put it that way."

She stared directly into his eyes, the sensation making her feel heady and awkward, as if her limbs were going to refuse to support her at any moment.

"How would you put it, then?" she asked softly.

"I'm simply repaying a debt, paying tribute to a man who once helped me when I needed it badly. Oliver."

She stared at him quietly for several seconds. "The man we talked about. He was obviously a genuinely good person."

"He was more than good. He took me off the streets and gave me a chance."

Helena frowned. "What streets? Not Sloane's Cove. You aren't from here."

"No. I was only here once. My mother came here on a trip with a...friend, a man, when I was twelve. She and I, well, let's just say we weren't close. I was pretty much expected to survive on my own for the most part, so I did. Along the way, I ran into Oliver. I believe I was lifting his keys at the time. He lifted them right back."

"Didn't he report you to the police?"

Jackson smiled. "He should have. Instead, he took me on, gave me my start. He arranged for me to go to a good school."

His voice had dipped low.

"He was like a father to you."

Jackson's laugh was automatic. "Yes, and there's no way I made it easy for him. I was wild."

"But now you're not."

He turned those dark silvery eyes on her and Helena knew that she was wrong. The wildness was still there. It simply lay beneath the surface, controlled. Jackson was no tame puppy.

"I was overseas when Oliver died," he said simply. "I haven't really had a chance to say goodbye. When I do, I want to do it right. To give three other people the kind of chance he gave me. To do something good in his name. It's past time."

Helena tipped back her head, studying him, the seriousness of his expression. The words hadn't flowed smoothly from him. His voice had been cool, but his lashes had flickered, as if this wasn't easy for him. It probably wasn't. Jackson had come to say his final farewell to his friend. This would be a difficult time for him. The fact that he was going to turn something sad into something wonderful for the people she cared about touched her deeply.

She stepped down off the last step to stand beside Jackson. The warmth of the sun-shot path filtered through the soles of her shoes.

"What are you thinking?" Jackson asked as they began to carefully make their way toward the boulder-strewn shore where the scent of pine and sea mingled.

"I'm wondering why you're telling me all this."

"Because I think you know people and care about them. I need to know about them as well, more than I can get from mere public records. More than I can obviously get from simply asking a lot of questions and making everyone suspicious. I need to know what makes them tick, what their dreams are, their fears. I need someone to help me figure all that out without revealing my intentions."

"That's a tall order for anyone."

She looked up to find Jackson smiling lazily. "What?" she asked.

"Alma says you're big on tall orders. You're interested in just causes."

"Well, of course I'm interested."

Jackson raised a brow. "Exactly. You already know all the things I need to know."

"Maybe I do, but I couldn't choose one friend over another."

He shook his head. "I wouldn't expect you to. I only want you to help me see the citizens of Sloane's Cove through your eyes, to introduce them to me in a more intimate way than I could hope to achieve myself."

"And you really mean to help some of them?"

"I'm going to do some entertaining, to mingle as much as I can, to get to know people and their needs. In three weeks, at the tribute, I'll announce the three recipients in Oliver's memory. I'll carry on what he started."

Helena turned to walk backward to face him. The wind blew her hair back over her shoulders. "And you're going to let me be a part of this?"

"I'm hoping you'll agree."

He looked suddenly uncertain, and Helena wondered why this successful businessman, this man of the world, this fabulously handsome man should ever doubt his welcome. It was a dangerous train of thought to follow for a woman who had always been too impetuous.

She smiled up at him, stopped and reached up to place one palm against his jaw. Immediately she was swept into his heat and magnetism. It was all she could do to open her mouth and speak.

"I'd love to help you help someone, Jackson."

He placed his hand over her own, whether to pull away or to hold her there, Helena couldn't tell.

She could feel the deep breath that he took.

"This will mean spending more time together than I'd anticipated," he confessed.

"I suppose it will," she said.

"We may find ourselves in somewhat intimate settings at times. We won't always be separated by the kitchen."

She swallowed hard.

"I don't live in the kitchen twenty-four hours a day."

He smiled slightly. "I'm only trying to assure you that I meant what I told your brothers. Your welfare will be of utmost concern to me. I won't do anything that would jeopardize your health or your well-being. I won't let anything or anyone hurt you or your baby. That includes me."

His voice had dropped to a near whisper.

She nodded. "I trust you."

His chuckle was low and self-deprecating as he released her and stepped away. "Good. Keep trusting me. Knowing that you do will make it easier for me to resist touching you."

Her eyes opened wide. "Would you mind running that past me again?"

"Sorry, I'd rather not. And I want you to know that it's not something you need to worry about. I meant what I said when I told your brothers I'd keep you safe. Still, it's only fair to be honest about it, since I'm asking you to hire on for something you hadn't anticipated." He stared down at her. "You can change your mind. We can go back to the original plan or even no plan at all if you wish."

"And what will you do with no partner in crime, no cook?"

He didn't hesitate even a second. "I'll survive. I'm a rich, powerful man. You won't need to worry."

But she would. Rich and powerful didn't buy a man everything, and she had a strong suspicion that Jackson had missed out on many things in life. Maybe she was being naive, but she wondered how many people he knew who stood beside him no matter the risk. After all, he had come to Sloane's Cove alone.

She stepped closer. It was all she could do to open her mouth and speak.

"I'd be honored to help you, Jackson."

For half a second he stared into her eyes as if to assess her sincerity. She'd just bet that a man with his looks and in his position dealt with insincerity on an hourly basis.

Finally the tight muscles in his jaw relaxed. "Then we'll be partners in this venture together?" he asked.

She smiled and nodded. "And don't worry, Jackson. I understand the need for secrecy. If people knew, they'd be uncomfortable and tense. They wouldn't be themselves with you. So how will we go about this?"

He stared out at the water where the men were checking their lobster traps.

"I'll want you to introduce me to people and to tell me their stories. I think we'll need to be a bit more public. Will that be a problem for you?"

She furrowed her brow, not sure what he meant.

"With your brothers?" he added.

Helena wanted to laugh. She remembered Lilah's words earlier today. She remembered the look on her brothers' faces each time they'd encountered Jackson.

Would it be a problem for her to be constantly seen

in the company of a man who was made for women the way caviar was made for champagne?

No matter what kind of a pact they'd seemed to make with Jackson, it would be a problem. Her brothers were still smarting over the fact that they hadn't been able to foresee or to protect her from her experience with Peter. And Peter had been a very tame man.

Jackson wasn't Peter. He wasn't tame.

If she started whispering with Jackson in cozy corners, there'd be problems. On many fronts.

"Everything will be fine," she said, batting away her thoughts.

"If there's trouble, it's not your fault and it's not your problem. I'll handle it," Jackson told her, that rich, deep voice thrumming through her body.

She could have told him he was too late. There was already trouble if the mere sound of his voice could excite her.

But that was okay. She was forewarned and she was braced. Let the trouble begin.

It was important to keep reminding herself that she was here to do business, Helena thought the next evening, as she looked around the Coveside Restaurant, the site of her first public outing with Jackson. She'd suggested this place because it was a good spot to people watch, because it was her favorite and because, for some reason she couldn't quite explain, she wanted this town she loved to shine in Jackson's eyes. The Coveside was right on the water, with an outdoor area where you could sit by the sea and breathe in the rich, salty air. There was weathered wood planking beneath tables covered in navy-and-white gingham. Water glasses of yellow and white daisies shared space with fat light blue candles on each table. The restaurant was a cozy, rustic place during the daytime, but as the sun began to drift low in the sky, turning the horizon to lavender and pink and dusky blue, it was, she realized, a bit more romantic than she'd remembered.

She hoped Jackson wasn't thinking the same thing and wondering why she'd brought him here.

"Great seafood," she said suddenly, placing her silverware on her empty plate. She couldn't help but notice that Jackson had eaten every morsel of his meal, too.

A crooked grin lifted his lips and one brow rose. "Great seafood in Maine? Why, Helena, love, wherever did you find this place?"

Helena's sense of unease vanished and she chuckled. "Okay, you're right. That was a silly comment. I suppose I'm just terribly aware that you haven't been here since you were twelve, and that you're observing everything with new eyes. I guess where Sloane's Cove is concerned, I'm like an overprotective mother who wants everyone to think her baby is pretty."

He tilted his head in acknowledgment. "Don't worry, Helena. I assure you, your baby *is* pretty. The last time I was here, I was too young to really notice or care, but I can see now why people like to summer in Maine."

"And winter somewhere else," she admitted.

He studied her expression. "What's it like then?"

She grinned. "My grandmother used to say that it would put thick, curly hair on a woman's chest."

He raised both brows and grinned. "Really? That cold?"

"Blustery," she confirmed. "A fair amount of the people I knew growing up have moved away. They want to be somewhere more lively in the winter."

"But not you."

She raised her chin. "I love it here."

She said that a bit too loudly with a tiny trace of defensiveness in her tone, and Jackson studied her intently.

A trace of guilt threaded its way through Helena. The man was, after all, here for just a few weeks. He was here to do a good thing, and he certainly wasn't responsible for the men who had walked away from Sloane's Cove and away from her. Or for her husband who had wanted to walk away.

"Sorry," she said a bit sheepishly.

"For what? For loving your hometown? Don't be sorry. I may not understand that kind of deep connection to any place or person, but I would never criticize such loyalty. It's refreshing."

"You felt a connection to Oliver."

"When a person saves your life, you're grateful."

He said it so simply, as if he had no real feeling for the man who had once helped him. Helena wondered why, because it was clear by the intensity of his gaze, and the simple fact that he was here doing this, that he cared. She supposed that he was still aching at Oliver's death, still angry about it. It hadn't been that long ago, and she remembered full well her own anger when her parents had died.

Without hesitation, knowing that it was dangerous to touch, Helena slid her hand across the table. She covered Jackson's big hand with her own.

"You cared for him," she said simply.

He studied her. "I'm not much of a man for strong feelings, Helena."

She could swear his words were a warning. She'd be wise to heed them, but she knew he'd felt something important for Oliver Davis. Otherwise he wouldn't be going to so much trouble when he had a business to run.

"Oliver helped you," she insisted, "and once you make your decision here, people will want to make a connection to you, too. They'll be grateful," she said, using his own words. She deliberately avoided mentioning the details of what his decision entailed. They were sitting off on their own, but there was always the chance that someone would wander near, and Helena understood that giving away Jackson's plans would complicate matters.

Jackson tensed at her touch. He stared directly into her eyes and shook his head slowly. "I don't want that. I'm not doing this for any other reason than to honor Oliver. Don't be fooled into thinking that I'm anything like him. Oliver is the man who started everything, and he's the man who deserves the credit. I'll be back at my business, back on my travels, as soon as I've completed my goal here. Everything that needs to be done can be done long-distance."

There was a message in his eyes, and that message was very clear. *Don't get too close to me.* Helena might have blushed if she hadn't worried about what turned a man like Jackson, who traveled constantly and met new people repeatedly, into such a loner. She knew so little, only that he'd once been a child who'd been mistreated by his own mother.

She wanted to close her eyes at the thought, to do all she could to protect the life growing within her.

"Well, hel-lo, Jackson. I wondered when I'd run into you." The voice sounded behind Jackson and Helena glanced up into the face of a man who looked like a golden angel but whose smile was just a touch too smug to be angelic.

Jackson didn't turn. "Hello, Barrett," he said coolly. "What brings you here?"

The man laughed and sent a smile Helena's way as he moved closer. "Do you need to ask? How tiresome. But if you must know, I'm here with Emil Ramsey, a client I'm courting and my new best friend. He was almost your client once, I believe."

"That's interesting, Bar."

Barrett laughed again, a flat, tinny sound.

"Still can't get a rise out of you, can I, Jack? I always did assume that underneath all that skin the women find so pleasing that you were pure stone. Or ice. It makes a man wonder just what kind of parents you had, doesn't it?"

Jackson simply stared, unblinking.

Finally Barrett shrugged. "All right, I'll get to the point. I heard about all those delightfully rich people pouring into this area and I couldn't help thinking what a feast of possibilities this would be for business. All those members of the elite in a good mood, on vacation and ready to spend their money. Besides, Emil wants to come to your party. He's convinced that anyone who's anyone will be here, and you know Emil. He wants to be noticed. He needs some good media coverage. So we flew in to court some potential new customers and do a little business for the next few weeks. While I'm here, I'll make the rounds of the coastal towns to scope out some product for my other clients. Then we'll finish with your blowout tribute to Oliver. I understand that no invitation is needed," he said with a fixed smile.

"It's open to the public, Barry. You can tell Emil that I won't have him thrown out, if that's what you're after here."

"Good enough. Would be bad for my business, you know."

Jackson didn't bat an eye. "Don't let us keep you from your dinner, Barrett," he said pointedly. It was clear that Jackson intended to end the conversation at that.

"Oh, but I'm not done talking. Not nearly. Aren't you going to introduce me to this beautiful lady you're with, or are you keeping her a secret?"

"Barry," Jackson drawled, "why on earth would I want to keep anything a secret from you?"

"Because I'm your biggest competitor, Jack? Because I irritate you? Because you wish I didn't exist?"

Jackson held out his hands, palms up. "I'm not going to spar with you, Barrett."

"And I'm not going to go away just because you wish I would. What fun would that be when it's so much more pleasant to stick around and bother you? It's always a true challenge to see if I can get a rise out of you. You're so self-controlled. And yet...you were Oliver's favorite."

Jackson shifted slightly. "Goodbye, Barrett."

The man turned his back on Jackson, but he didn't leave. Instead he directed his attention to Helena, smiling brilliantly. "Allow me to introduce myself, since Jack hasn't. I'm Barrett Richards and Jack's a bit…possessive about his ladies,'' he confided. He reached out and took her hand, smoothing his own hand across her fingers a bit too intimately.

Helena felt her breath trap in her throat. She tried a weak smile.

"Helena Austin,'' she said. "I work for Mr. Castle.''

The man dared to raise one brow.

"Keep that up, and you'll be swallowing all those exquisitely capped teeth,'' Jackson said dryly. "Ms. Austin is a very talented cook.''

Barrett gave her a long, slow smile. "Looks like I should have scoped out the help in person,'' he said, raising Helena's fingers to his lips. "I happen to be a connoisseur of good food and lovely women, but my cook is, unfortunately, merely passable and a man at that. Perhaps we can meet and…talk someday soon, Ms. Austin.''

The man's eyes raked over her, and Helena felt a somewhat childish urge to snatch her hand away and cover herself with her napkin. Instead she simply nodded.

"Goodbye, Jack,'' the man said with a laugh. "I'm sure we'll see more of each other. Maybe we'll even have a little business competition while we're here. I do love a good contest, especially with a worthy opponent, and you were always that, although you never were much of a man for sharing your treasures with other men, were you?''

He arched one brow and bent over Helena's hand. His lips touched her skin in a practiced gesture.

"Goodbye, Ms. Austin. It's been a delight to make your acquaintance. I'll look forward to meeting with you again. Maybe without a steely-eyed chaperon next time.''

He winked at her and walked away.

Silence reigned at the table for several seconds.

''Well…that went pretty well, don't you think?'' Helena managed to say. ''I don't see any blood on the tablecloth, anyway.''

Jackson raised his head. He lifted those long, thick lashes of his and showed her silvery eyes that held a hint of a glow. ''You're a gem, Helena,'' he told her with a rising smile.

''I'm sorry,'' she said. ''None of this is my business, I know, but why does that man dislike you so much?''

A mask descended over Jackson's eyes. ''We go back a bit. When he was twenty-three, Barrett was an opportunistic young man trying to make a name for himself in the business world. He apparently learned of Oliver's generosity and did his best to get in his good graces. But Oliver was a good judge of character. He resisted Barrett's attempts to get money from him. Still, he believed in giving people a second chance and so, eventually, he sent Barrett to me for a job. It didn't work out as he'd planned.''

''Jackson?''

He took her hand that Barrett had kissed. ''Don't worry, Helena. Barrett won't be a problem for me— or for you.''

''But you're both here, and in a town this small, you'll bump into each other time and again.''

He shrugged, called for the check and paid the bill. He took Helena's arm as they exited the restaurant, and they walked down near the shore. ''We're not here for the same reasons, so it shouldn't matter.

What Barrett wants and what I want are completely different.''

"What do you want?"

"I'm not here to compete with him, if that's what you mean. Once my business here is completed, I'll leave. I'm not one to linger. When something's over, I fade away."

He said those words as if he'd said them a thousand times. Helena didn't doubt that he'd done just that...every time a woman started getting too close. She wondered if he was saying them now to warn her off. Not that she needed any warning. She was responsible for another life now. She couldn't act irresponsibly. Besides, warning explosions had been going off inside her ever since she'd turned yesterday morning to find a half-naked, morning-sexy Jackson standing in the sunlight. She wondered how many women had awakened to brush that black satin hair from his eyes and give him a kiss filled with everything a woman had to offer, only to realize that he'd donned that I-don't-want-to-hurt-you look. Probably too many. Good thing she wouldn't become one of them.

Helena tried for a halfway sassy smile as Jackson helped her to a seat on a smooth, chair-size boulder. "So you do your job and then move on to the next one? Is that what's made you such a success?"

He held out his hands in a gesture of acceptance. "It's always a kick to find the right product for the right customer. It was from the day I first met a man looking for a picture to hang in his den and I went out and found someone willing to paint a fantasy picture of his horse winning the Kentucky Derby. It's a challenge, almost a game at times. Isn't that the way you feel about finding the right ingredient to make a recipe more special, or matching a meal to a customer's tastes?''

''You understand,'' she said, realizing that he felt the same thrill of the hunt that she did. ''But how does Barrett fit into the picture? He seems to delight in baiting you.''

Jackson blew out a breath as he looked out into the waves. ''Barrett's a fly,'' he finally said. ''An annoyance. Yes, he is my competitor, and not a bad one at that. He *does* deliver what he says he will, but he doesn't truly take the time to look at the big picture. The customer's satisfaction is short-lived. He's also willing to procure things I don't deal in, so even though we do compete in a sense, we often don't overlap our business. You don't have to worry about Barrett.''

His last words seemed to take on a deeper meaning, and Helena had the feeling that they were talking about more than Jackson's business concerns. When he quickly changed the subject and complimented her on her choice of a restaurant, she was pretty sure the man was trying to distract her.

''Tell me about that man over there,'' he told her, switching the subject and nodding back toward the restaurant where an old man occupied a table overlooking the water. The man was alone, drinking cup after cup of coffee.

''Is this the way we're going to do it?'' she asked with a small laugh. ''I'm going to slowly introduce you to each and every one of the citizens of Sloane's Cove?''

''We'll have to work faster than that,'' he conceded, ''or I'll have a beard as long and gray as his by the time we're done. No, we're going to do a little entertaining, you and I, a lot of objective studying of lists, but it wouldn't hurt to do a little of the hands-on stuff when we run into people as well. Does that suit you?"

"You're the boss," she said lightly.

"But I'm in your lovely hands, Helena," he pointed out.

A deep shiver ran through her at the sound of his voice. "Well, in that case, we'll begin," she said. "That happens to be Elliott Woodford. He's a former sailor turned teacher, and since he retired, he runs a small historical museum. He's a widower. He's also a total sweetheart. All the ladies in town want him, but he's announced that he'll never marry again. His heart's with his wife in heaven."

"Sounds sad."

Helena shook her head. "Not really. He's happy, and he keeps himself busy and contented knowing she's waiting for him."

"I take it he doesn't need my help."

"No, I don't think he does, but that doesn't mean you both wouldn't benefit from meeting each other. I think you'd like each other. You might have a lot in common."

"Because we're both loners?"

"Maybe, and also because you both know what you want out of life. You're very...certain."

"You don't know what you want?"

She studied him for a few seconds. "No, I do. I want to stay here, feed people, write cookbooks and raise my child. And, when it comes down to it, I'm a bit of a loner, too."

"Not for long," he said, looking down to where her child lay nestled inside her.

"No, I guess you're right."

"You may want someone to help you raise your baby. You may change your mind and find you want a man."

"I—I don't think so. No," she said, almost too quickly, fumbling for the words.

As Jackson stared down at her with dark, questioning eyes, Helena hoped that she was right, and that his words didn't come true. Because the only man she seemed to have the slightest interest in right now was him.

Chapter Four

Telling Helena she needed a man had been a stupid thing to say, Jackson couldn't help thinking as he lay in his bed that night, his arms behind his head, mulling over the day. He had clearly upset the lady, and she had a right to be upset. He was overstepping his boundaries as her employer, intruding into a private matter.

But he knew why he'd said it. She'd been sitting there looking lovelier than the day. Her voice had been tinged with admiration and genuine affection when she'd spoken of the elderly man in the restaurant. She'd seemed so untainted and unique. And Barrett Richards was going to try to make a conquest of her.

Jackson knew it as well as he knew the rhythm of the days. He knew it as well as he knew his business.

And while she might think she didn't like the man right now, Barrett knew how to change a woman's mind. He knew how to charm when he wanted to. He was a chameleon capable of becoming anything for a short time. Jackson had seen it happen with his own wife. He was pretty certain that Barrett convinced even himself of his sincerity at times.

The man would make a point of seeking out Helena, just as Jackson would make a point of protecting her. That was going to make doing simple business with the lady a bit more difficult.

He was already having to warn himself away from sliding his fingers into her silky-looking hair. He was forcing himself to resist taking her arm to help her keep her balance when she walked across a room. If he had to spend time in close quarters with her to guard her from Barrett's advances, there was no way he could convince himself that he didn't want to fold her into his arms every time he looked at her.

That was why he'd made that comment. He was trying to remind himself that he needed to leave her alone.

But that didn't mean he'd stopped wanting to taste her lips.

When it came down to the truth, he wasn't much better than Barrett after all.

That was his first thought when he woke up the next morning to the sound of the doorbell ringing. He passed into the kitchen and found Helena furiously trying to arrange things on the stove so that she could get the door and still not burn his breakfast. She was practically dancing from foot to foot. This couldn't be good for a woman in her condition.

"Don't worry, Helena, I can manage the door."

Her smile was better than any food he'd ever eaten. He skimmed past her into the living room, and when he swung back the white-paneled door, it was to greet a young Adonis standing on his porch. Beach-boy blue eyes, golden hair swept back by the breeze and a sleeveless sweatshirt that revealed muscles that could have been attained only by hours at the gym.

The guy gave Jackson a wide, confident smile. "Helena home?"

Jackson lifted one brow. "Are you another one of the Austin brothers?"

The man snorted. "No way. I'm just here to see the lady. The name's Keith. She'll know who I am."

His air indicated that she would also like the fact that he was here. Something unpleasantly rough and thick seemed to fill up Jackson's chest. It was a sensation he didn't want to analyze or get used to, so he nodded the young man in and strode to the kitchen.

"Keith is here to see you," he said dryly. "Would you like me to take over here?"

"Keith? Not Keith Garlan?"

"I wouldn't know that, angel," Jackson said in a low voice he tried to keep even. "The man's got blond hair, blue eyes, muscles. Seems to think you'll be glad to see him. Ring a bell?"

Helena frowned. She wiped her hands on her white chef's apron embroidered with poppies and bluebonnets. It was a generously full apron, concealing most of the front of her, but for some strange reason, it seemed incredibly...sexy. The apron started at the high curve of her breasts, making Jackson wish he could wrap his arms around her, flick open the ties and slide the thin cotton right down to reveal those soft curves. Didn't matter that she was clothed beneath it. A man knew what he would find there. For some strange reason, Jackson didn't want Keith thinking those same thoughts.

"I'll be right back," she said, almost breathless, a small frown creasing her brow. She deposited a plate of banana pancakes on the table and arranged orange juice, coffee and maple syrup for him. "Please. Eat," she said, taking a deep breath.

She smoothed her hands down the apron again, causing Jackson to concentrate on those sweet, luscious curves. He didn't sit—or eat.

Helena frowned. "I'm sorry. I shouldn't be receiving guests at your house," she said. "I'll just go send him away."

And instantly Jackson felt angry at himself for bringing more worry to her life at a time when she needed to be serene.

"You're doing your job beautifully, Helena," he said. "I don't mind if you have guests."

"So sit," she said, but he still stood. He reached out and slid his arms around either side of her. The warmth and nearness of her was intoxicating. Her soft scent of vanilla and maple and sweet woman's flesh drifted to him, making him feel as though he'd like nothing better than to lay her on his bed, taste his fill this minute and for hours afterward. Instead he snagged the ties of her apron, pulled gently and released her. He peeled back the enveloping covering and lifted it from her, revealing the pale yellow dress she wore beneath. She was still more tempting than any woman had a right to be, but at least the arrogant male standing in the living room wouldn't be entertaining visions of doing what he himself was doing right now.

"Wouldn't want to greet your guest in your work clothes," he said, trying to keep his voice steady.

She took a deep breath, lifting her breasts, soft

color suffusing her skin and turning her neck a delectable, edible peach.

Deliberately Jackson forced himself to sit. "See, I'm fine," he said. "Go."

She looked down to where he'd placed her apron on the counter, as if she wanted to cover herself with it again. But she didn't pick it up. Instead, she nodded. She left the room.

Jackson closed his eyes. He wondered what demonic things he must have done in some past life to deserve this kind of torture, but he knew it wasn't former deeds that were haunting him. It was the here and now, the Helena part of his life.

As he took the first bite of the best pancakes he'd ever eaten, he wished that Helena were older or less attractive. He'd be able to concentrate on enjoying his food a lot more if that were the case.

Instead, he was going to spend the next few minutes wondering who the hell Keith was and what he wanted with Helena Austin.

Helena folded her fingers against her side as she hurriedly left the room. For a moment there, when Jackson had been close against her, the warmth of his arms encircling her, she'd thought she might just do something completely unacceptable. Like wrap her arms around his neck, like ask him to please kiss her, like faint.

But now she had to be more clearheaded. There was only one reason that she could think of that Keith Garlan would be seeking her out today, and it was not a good one.

"Hey, babe," he said as she entered the living

room. "Bill told me I'd find you here bright and early. He's a good man."

Good old Bill, Helena thought, pasting on a weak smile and plotting her oldest brother's slow and torturous demise.

"Any particular reason you wanted to see me, Keith?"

He shrugged. "Always like seeing you, Helena. You know that, but I also thought I'd swing by and let you know that your brothers aren't too happy that you're spending after-hours time with him," he said, nodding his head toward the kitchen. "Everybody knows he goes through women the way other men go through beer. You've got a baby to think about. You need someone more reliable. Someone who belongs here in Sloane's Cove."

Helena gritted her teeth. "Well, I thank you for your concern, Keith, but there's really nothing to worry about. Mr. Castle and I have a number of things to consult about. I assure you he has no interest in me."

"Yeah. Right. That's why he looked at me like I was a worm when he opened the door. Doesn't like the fact that you and I might be planning something right now, either."

"But we're not."

"Could be we are. I've always liked you, Helena."

His tone was sincere, and Helena sighed. Keith was a nice man, but what he wanted was a nice, pliable woman on his own terms. He wanted a woman to give all she had to him, and Helena wasn't giving away bits and pieces of herself anymore. Besides, the truth was she liked Keith, but she didn't *more* than like him. Still, she knew better than to be quite so honest.

"I'm just not interested in dating right now, Keith, and you can tell Bill that I said so."

"You might change your mind. I might persuade you to." He took a step forward. Helena took a step back.

As if she'd rung a bell calling for help, a shadow appeared in the doorway. "Introduce me to your friend, Helena," Jackson commanded as he entered the room.

A rush of pure gratitude washed over her. She opened her mouth to speak, but Keith held up one hand.

"We've already met, I thought, and anyway, I have to get to work," the young man said. "I'll wait, Helena," he added. "I'm the kind of man you want. I'd be good for you and the baby. I'd provide for you, and I wouldn't compare you to other women."

He aimed his parting shot Jackson's way as he jammed a baseball cap on his head and sailed out the door and down the steps, hopping over the door of his convertible into the seat. When the car was down the road, Jackson turned to Helena.

"Maybe I owe you an apology?"

She smiled slightly and shook her head. "My brothers think I need a husband. I have a feeling that Keith is just the first of any number of suitors who'll be calling. I'll talk to the boys, but I doubt it will do any good. Austins are incredibly pigheaded, and it appears that my brothers think you have dishonorable intentions toward me. I'm sorry. It's so silly. I'll do my best to tell them they're wrong."

She had walked up close to him as she spoke. She was looking up earnestly into his eyes, sorry that she'd brought this complication into his life. "I'll tell them today," she promised.

He reached out and cupped his hand around her jaw. He slid his other hand behind her back and slowly, deliberately drew her near.

"Don't tell them," he said, his voice a low ribbon of sound in the quiet of the morning. "They may be right." And he brought his lips down on hers. He tasted of syrup and heat and masculinity. His mouth covered hers, claimed hers, seared her with the longing to have him pull her closer still. She could feel his big palm splayed against her back, urging her against him as he kissed her once, twice and yet again.

And then she was free. He was steadying her on her feet. He was stepping back.

"My apologies," he said, his voice less than even as it shimmied across her senses. "But as I said, your brothers seem to be right. I may want to treat you with the utmost respect due a loyal employee, but I tend to be…unpredictable. You seem to have that effect on me. I'll do my best to control it from here on out, and to stay out of your way when your suitors come to call."

An ache started deep inside Helena. Jackson was looking as if he wanted to take a swing at someone, and she had a feeling that it was himself he wanted to slug. She wished she could go back and reclaim the last few moments. Then she wouldn't know what it was like to be kissed by Jackson Castle. She wouldn't be longing for him to do it again. He wouldn't be wishing she'd hurry up and get out of his life and his house. He'd stop beating up on himself.

She shook her head. "This is your house. There's no need to apologize."

Dark silver eyes looked deep into her own. It took only that for her to remember the feel of his flesh, the taste of his lips.

"I don't—" she began, looking down at herself. "I'm not sure I understand."

"Nothing to understand. You're a very desirable woman. I'm a very tempted man."

She smiled then, couldn't help it. "You must be worrying about your business here more than I'd thought. That must be affecting your eyesight and your judgment if you're equating me with desirable. I'm—well, just look. I'm awfully pregnant, Jackson." She nearly crossed her eyes looking down at her stomach, and when she looked up again his scowl had faded, replaced by the slightest of grins.

"Try looking up into a mirror, darlin', rather than down at your toes. You're a temptation, Helena, and I'm definitely tempted beyond what is wise. This just wouldn't do, you know, you and I, because you— well, you *are* pregnant. You don't need a temporary man."

Something a bit painful moved through her just then. She shrugged it away.

"I don't need a man at all," she said forcefully.

"Looks like that's going to be a problem, then."

She followed the direction of his gaze. Another car was coming down the road and pulling into the drive. She recognized the driver and groaned.

"Bob Mason," she said. "Frank must have sent him."

"You need me?" Jackson asked quietly.

She almost said yes. She had a fierce urge to say

yes, she needed him very badly. To kiss her again, to make her feel like a desirable woman when she hadn't felt like that for a very long time. But he was right. Jackson and her, it just wasn't wise.

"I'll manage," she said.

But she noticed that he didn't move too far down the hall.

She could feel his presence. Her very body was tingling with the sense that Jackson was near, near enough to keep her restless and wanting.

Chapter Five

Helena had more energy than anyone on the verge of having a baby should rightfully have, Jackson couldn't help thinking two days later as he watched her make lists, pull out recipes and study information sheets on the locals.

"This is such an adventure," she said, passing by the doorway as she worked, a pink-and-white apron hiding her from his view again. "Let's have the Leggits and the Brannigans over tomorrow if they're available. Sharon Leggit is the youngest of seven and her parents are already strapped trying to send her brothers and sisters to school. I'm afraid Sharon is going to get married just to take the pressure off her family. She volunteers at the animal shelter when she can and she really wants to be a veterinarian, but it may never happen if things don't change. And the Brannigans are the first people to offer help to someone in need even though they have major medical concerns themselves. Or maybe they're too old. You might be only looking for young people." Helena's voice drifted in from the next room. Then she walked through the doorway carrying a heavy tea tray.

Jackson felt smoke building up inside him.

"Do not do that again," he told her, taking the tray from her.

"I'm sorry. I suspected you were mostly looking for younger recipients, but I was just throwing out ideas."

For half a second he didn't know what she was talking about. She looked genuinely stricken and contrite.

"I know it's your money and your project. Sometimes I just get carried away."

Jackson took her by the hand. He waltzed her backward slightly until she was up against a chair.

"Sit. Please," he told her, gazing directly into her eyes.

She gazed right back. She sat and he grabbed an ottoman and pushed it in front of the chair. Carefully he lifted her legs, smoothing her skirt down over her knees and trying not to notice the feel of her skin as he settled her in. Trying to stem the urge to slide his fingers beneath her skirt and up that long length of delicious thigh.

He cleared his throat, stuffed his hands into his back pockets. Like a kid, he thought. He was acting like a kid in more ways than one.

"I wasn't referring to the Brannigans, Helena," he said gently. "If you think they're people we could help, then naturally I'd want to try. I trust your judgment."

"You do? I'm glad, Jackson."

She sat forward eagerly in the chair, ready to stand if he'd let her, he was sure.

He leaned forward, placing his hands on the arms of the chair, pinning her there.

"I do," he agreed softly. "What I don't trust is that you won't overwork yourself. My complaints don't have anything to do with the plans for the Leggits and the Brannigans. I just don't want you lifting any heavy trays."

She smiled consolingly. "It's really not that heavy. Why, an—"

"Ant could lift it," he finished. "I know. So you've told me. Nevertheless, when you have any trays to carry, or baskets to carry, or bags to carry, I want you to do something for me."

She raised one suspicious brow. "I'm the employee. It's *my* job," she argued.

"And I'm the employer. It's not your job unless I say so. I'm perfectly capable of helping you."

"It's not necessary."

She opened her mouth to argue further. He gently placed his fingers beneath her chin, silencing her.

"It's very necessary, Helena," he whispered. He stroked his hand upward and she closed her mouth. Their eyes met, held, and he eased back. "All right?"

"I wouldn't do anything to risk my child, Jackson, but all right, I'll call you if I need something carried," she agreed, but he was just betting that she would forget their agreement the very next time she got busy in the kitchen. Helena had a tendency to want to do for others at an expense to herself, he was realizing.

No wonder her brothers were having no trouble finding suitors to send to his door. Another young puppy had showed up this morning. Jackson had cheerfully answered the door half dressed, with shaving cream on his face.

Helena had shot a curious look at his half-naked state, then kindly sent the young man on his way.

This was not how he'd envisioned himself spending his time when he'd planned this trip to Sloane's Cove. But he was glad that he was there. He didn't want to see her unhappy. He didn't want to see her marrying just anybody. When the right man showed up, he'd back off if Helena wanted him to. Until then, he considered it his solemn duty as her employer to look over every young man who dared to make a play for her.

"Jackson?" she was asking.

He shook his head free of his thoughts and glanced down at her, questioning.

"About tomorrow night," she began.

"The Leggits and the Brannigans," he agreed. "They're the ones?"

"They're possibilities," she corrected. "You'll decide which ones you want, of course. I'll just provide the background material and the food."

He knew she'd provide more. She'd run around serving everyone the way she served him. She'd consider it her solemn responsibility to make sure the conversation didn't lag. She'd run herself ragged—if he let her.

Half an hour later he let himself out the door. When he returned, he had something to make things a little easier.

"It's just a serving cart," he said when she exclaimed.

"Right. It's the Cadillac of serving carts, Jackson," she said, pulling out all the drawers and examining the carved burnished oak top. "You didn't have to do this. It's not like you need one or that it's the kind of thing you'll be able to bring home with you on the plane."

"You need it. It'll keep you from lifting too much."

"You don't trust me to ask for your help."

He gave her a wide grin and leaned forward, his lips next to her ear.

"No, I don't," he whispered.

Her silken taffy-colored hair brushed his lips. She took a visible deep breath. "Oh, well then, thank you," she whispered back, turning her head.

And now her lips were next to his. Her breath was warm on his face. He closed the gap, brushed her lips softly with his own, made the mistake of touching her.

"Don't thank me. Just take care of yourself—and the baby," he said.

She nodded slowly.

"And Helena?"

"Yes?"

"If I ever get this close to you again, I want you to do something."

"What?"

"Slap my face."

Her eyes widened, and then a smile formed. "I hardly think it's appropriate for a woman to slap her employer."

"I hardly think it's appropriate for an employer to kiss his cook."

"We were sealing a pact. You were giving me a gift. We were finalizing the deal."

He raised one brow. "Nice of you to let me off the hook."

"Jackson?"

"Yes?"

"It was a nice kiss. I'm not going to slap you if you do it again."

He groaned. "I think I'd better leave."

She smiled. "Oh, yes, I have tons of things to do if we're having guests tomorrow. Go tend to your business. We've got lots of craftsmen here on the island. No point in letting your competitors hog all the good stuff. Go hunt for some treasure."

But he knew he'd already found a treasure right here in his kitchen. Unfortunately, Helena was *forbidden* treasure.

Unfortunately, he'd been known to have a yen for things that were forbidden.

"Our Helena is a total sweetheart," Marie Brannigan was telling Jackson as Helena wheeled in the serving tray. "She stops in to check on Hugh and me at least once a week, just to make sure we're feeling up to par. She takes us to do our rounds at the hospital, too, when we need a ride. That's so important. There are so many people there who need comforting or just someone to visit with or talk to. Oh, that looks scrumptious, dear," she said as Helena placed a plate of braised summer vegetables and marinated chicken kabobs in front of her.

The woman was smiling in spite of her painfully gnarled fingers, the cane she kept at her side and the frayed appearance of her clothing, Jackson couldn't help noticing. She and her husband both looked frail, but Helena had told him that they visited the ill in the hospital without fail at least once a week in spite of the fact that they couldn't afford even the most basic transportation on their fixed incomes. And Helena, who was working full-time, writing a book and on the verge of giving birth, was driving them? Jackson wondered what other things he didn't know about his cook.

"They call Hugh and Marie the guardian angels at the hospital," Helena offered.

Jackson wondered what people called Helena.

"It's important work you do," he said to the couple.

"Oh, we just visit people," Marie said.

He nodded. "As I said, important work. If I'd had people like you to visit me the last time I was in the hospital, I might not have been such a bear to live with."

He rose to help Helena into her chair and she looked up at him, an expression of concern in her eyes. "Was it something serious? The reason you were in the hospital?"

A smile lifted his lips. "You can't go back and change history for me, much as you'd like to, Helena, and no it was nothing serious. A minor head wound from an automobile accident, Florence Nightingale."

"A minor head wound?" she asked, skepticism clouding her voice.

Sharon Leggit chuckled. "He's got your number already, Helena. But she's more than Florence Nightingale, Mr. Castle. When I was hyperventilating about having to make a speech in class, Helena coached me three days running until I could make the speech without even thinking about what I was saying."

"Hmpff," Helena said. "You most certainly did

know what you were saying. Sid Taylor told me that the teacher quizzed you on the material and you answered every question right. You earned that A all by yourself. And you did it while working a job after school and volunteering at the veterinary clinic.''

Jackson smiled. He wondered if Helena knew just how hard she was cheering for her friends. He was happy to see that when the meal was over, Sharon hopped up to help Helena and insisted that she and her sisters were taking care of all the cleanup chores in spite of Helena's protests that they were guests.

Of course, he knew that Helena was never going to let Sharon go through with her plan.

"Thank you, but I've got help coming in later this evening," he said before Helena could answer. "Ben, why don't you and your brother lend me a hand hustling these things into the kitchen so the ladies don't worry about the mess?"

Helena frowned.

Jackson wondered just how he was going to manage to hustle Helena home without her doing the dishes. He supposed he and Abe would have to have a talk before the next dinner party and see if there were any able high school students who could use a part-time job now and then. As it was, for tonight he was more than capable of taking care of cleanup duty. It wouldn't be the first time he'd made a mess and had to get out of it.

Helena opened her mouth.

"Don't worry about it," he said gently.

Hugh Brannigan laughed. "Might as well tell Helena not to breathe. She's been taking care of people's problems as long as I can remember. And being taken advantage of, too," he said, bristling. "Why, when I think of that young punk Larry Egan asking someone else to the prom after she'd spent six months convincing him that he wasn't a total loser, I just want to—''

His wife gently touched his hand and shushed him.

Helena was looking a bit pink and uncomfortable.

"That was a number of years ago, Hugh," she said gently. "I'm over it."

"I know. I know. But it wasn't the only time something like that happened. How about that time—"

His wife cleared her throat. "Another time, dear. You're embarrassing her," Marie said firmly.

Hugh looked up from his ranting. Jackson registered that fact even though his gaze was firmly planted on Helena. She was blushing sweetly, trying to smile but not quite succeeding.

So there were those who had taken advantage of her nature. It didn't surprise him. Not at all.

He was going to have to ask her about that, find out just who had hurt her.

She wouldn't like that.

And it wasn't wise. He'd promised to curb any feelings he had toward her. He knew the danger of getting involved. No, he wouldn't embarrass her by invading her privacy.

At least, not yet.

"I have to go out for a while later today," Helena told Jackson three days later. "Will that be all right?"

"More marketing? I'll come along to help you."

She gave him that I-don't-think-so look she usually reserved for her brothers. "Not marketing," she said. "And nothing where I'll be bench-pressing or anything of that nature," she promised.

"Is there something you need that I haven't provided? Something I can...help you with?"

She couldn't help chuckling and smiling down at her abdomen. "Not unless you've earned a medical degree in the last few hours. I have to go to the doctor, Jackson."

Instantly he took a deep breath. "Is there a problem?"

"No. No problem."

"You're healthy? You and the little one?"

"I think so."

"But you don't know that for sure."

"I'm pretty sure we're just fine and coming along in a timely fashion. The baby's kicking me on a regular basis. Turning somersaults, too. Everything seems pretty normal, I've been told. It's just a routine checkup, Jackson. That's what happens. I go in pretty frequently at this stage of the game."

He nodded, and she couldn't help noting that every time his gaze wandered down to her abdomen, it wandered away just as quickly. Clearly this man had a phobia about pregnancies.

"You're sure you're all right? It doesn't...hurt when the baby kicks? He's not in danger of breaking anything? Your skin? His leg? I don't know that much about the stages of pregnancy. No children, you know."

She knew, but she couldn't help thinking that on that show she'd seen they'd mentioned that he'd once been married.

"I'm exceptionally healthy," she assured him. "Healthy enough to go visit the rental agency about the tents we'll be needing for the day of the tribute to Oliver. I thought maybe I would go with you to visit the florist later today.''

"We'll see…after you see what the doctor says. I can always go alone.''

She frowned. "And leave me out of the fun? I don't think so, Jackson.''

"Do you always have this much energy?''

She nodded. "I seem to have even more lately than I used to. The first few months I was pregnant, I was tired, but lately I've gotten my second wind. I just might try a few somersaults myself.''

Jackson pinned her in place with a frown.

"I was kidding.''

"I think I know that, but if you're feeling energetic, you just might do something equally inadvisable. Maybe I should have a word with your doctor. He might have something to say about all these extra duties I've assigned you.''

She held up her hand, placed it on his chest.

"Don't.''

He stared down at where she touched him.

"No one's responsible for me but me, Jackson,'' she said quietly. "I can't afford to let other people start helping me make decisions. Once the baby comes, it'll be just the two of us. I'll have to be wise enough for two. I may have family and friends, but a lot of the time we'll be alone. I have to get used to doing things alone, making decisions alone.''

He stared at her for long seconds.

"You could marry. Your brothers want you to.''

"I don't want to. My husband—well, let's just say that I don't want to.''

"You still love him.''

She shook her head. "It wasn't that way for us,

and I'm not marrying again, not to please my brothers."

"But as you say, it's difficult for a woman alone with a baby. Somebody told me that once."

"Someone important?"

He shrugged. "My wife."

"She was telling you that she wanted you to stay?"

"She was telling me that she wanted a divorce so that she could marry the father of her child. I gave her what she wanted. And I'll concede on this issue to you, too. Go see your baby's doctor, Helena. I'll keep away any prospective daddies who show up while you're gone."

Helena studied him for long seconds, then he slowly lifted his lips in a heartbreakingly tender smile. He reached out and brushed her cheek with the backs of his fingers.

"Don't do that, Helena."

"What?"

"Start worrying about me. Don't start planning my salvation the way you plan everyone else's. I probably shouldn't have told you that last bit about my wife, because now it's worrying you. Don't let it. I'm not in love with the woman. I'm fine. I'm unaffected."

But if he was so unaffected, Helena thought as she drove herself to the doctor, why couldn't he even look at the place where her child lay?

Jackson might be over his wife, but he still had scars. He wasn't ever going to have a child to hold. He wasn't ever again going to trust another woman enough to commit to her forever.

Helena's heart contracted even as she realized that none of that should matter to her. She'd sworn off trying to save men she was attracted to, and she didn't have the power to change Jackson's past, anyway.

But surely she could do a little something that would demonstrate her appreciation for what he was doing for her hometown. She'd have to put some serious thought into this matter.

Chapter Six

"Whoa, the streets are certainly crowded today,"
Helena said as Jackson took her arm to keep her from
being jostled by the passing crowd the next day.
"Looks like you and your tribute to Oliver brought
in lots of business for the merchants. I've been told
to tell you that everyone is very grateful, even if
bringing business to Sloane's Cove wasn't your intent."

"Don't fool yourself, Helena. I've been enjoying
myself tremendously. I've never belonged to a town
before."

"You live in Boston."

"True, but I fly in and out on such a regular basis
that it's more like a place to crash between business
trips."

"Sounds tiring."

He grinned down at her. "I thrive on it. It's exciting."

She raised one brow, leaning back to study him.

"Tell me about it."

Jackson held out his hands, palms up. "A client tells me he's looking for something, but he's not sure what. Now it's my job to figure out what that something is and supply it, to find the treasure that will make the client sit up and purr."

"Difficult."

"Yes, it often is. But you'd be surprised at how often I find that the treasure people didn't even know they wanted was closer than anyone would have thought. An item someone was going to sell without realizing that they had a one-of-a-kind work of art. An unknown craftsman creating away in an apartment over a store three blocks from the client's house. A man can sometimes find beauty that's been hiding for years just below his line of sight," he whispered, his voice dipping low.

Helena looked up into Jackson's eyes, just *above* her line of sight.

"Are you trying to tell me something, Jackson?" she asked.

"Yes. You're a treasure of an employee, and you need to sit down."

She frowned. "No, I do not. We came out here today to meet a few of Sloane's Cove's finest. I'm working."

Jackson peered at his watch. "Not for much longer. Almost lunchtime. And you've already introduced me to quite a few people today."

"Hello, Mr. Castle," a woman called from across the street.

"Good morning, Ellen," Jackson replied. "I hope you find owners for all your adoptees today." The woman was walking four dogs, their leashes tangling as they tumbled about her feet.

"When you get back to Boston and you need a pet, just contact me. I'll find the perfect animal for you," the lady called back just before she turned the corner.

"Isn't she a wonder?" Helena asked. "She feeds those dogs out of her own pocket. And how about John Nesbith? He told me that you were kind to him."

"He's a great kid. Very industrious," Jackson admitted. "He's definitely got a bright future."

"He did a nice job of shining up your Alfa Romeo, didn't he? It was probably the highlight of his sixteen years. He's had a hard life."

Jackson chuckled. "I had to beg him to take money for the job. He told me that he considered it an honor just to be able to touch such a fine specimen of a car, that he couldn't think of anything more beautiful."

"Yes, well, give him a year or two. John hasn't done a lot of intersecting with the opposite sex, yet."

But she had, Jackson knew. Even if Hugh hadn't made those comments at dinner the other day, even if her brothers hadn't proven to be so suspicious, he would have known the truth. She got that pleased but wary look whenever he got too close. This lady had been hurt and she didn't want to be hurt again. He promised himself he wouldn't damage her in any way.

And that included getting her to slow down when the woman clearly only had a fast forward button. He wondered what a man would have to do to get Helena Austin to grow dreamy and languorous.

And when he'd learn not to think such thoughts...

"Come on," he said, taking her by the hand. "I have an idea."

"What kind of idea?"

"Don't sound so suspicious."

"I'm always suspicious when someone says 'I have an idea,' and they don't tell you what the idea is."

He could appreciate that. No one liked to be blind-sided.

He smiled down at her. "I was just thinking that we should take a bit of a breather. In the past few days I've met most of the people in the town. I've learned about their families, their backgrounds, their dreams. Yet you've been cooking for me for a week and a half now and I've never even had the chance to see any of your published work. I'd like to."

"You might be sorry about that. I tend to go a bit overboard once I get started talking about my writing."

Jackson chuckled. "You? Go overboard? Can't believe it, Helena. Now lead me on," he said, holding out his hands as if he meant for her to handcuff him.

Helena chuckled, too. "Okay, you asked for it. Don't say I didn't warn you. And no fair crying uncle if you're overcome with boredom."

She smiled and turned, her long hair breezing out about her, and Jackson moved to her side. His plan was working. He was finally going to get Helena to sit in a chair for more than five minutes.

He hoped.

"First, lunch," Helena said quietly as she led Jackson into her small blue cottage on her tree-lined street.

"No arguments here," Jackson said, noting the personal touches that made her house so like the woman. Warmth and color pervaded the living room. There was a crystal vase filled with red poppies and yellow daisies, yards of glass with the sun shining through, blue and yellow rag rugs strewn around the honey-oak floor.

"That's the plan," Helena whispered with a conspiratorial look. "I feed you until you're so stuffed you can't move and then I bring out my books and force you to admire them."

Her laughter was like a soothing waterfall, tea being served in a cool, forested glade. Jackson followed her into the kitchen.

"Let me help this time," he offered.

She started to shake her head, but he shushed her with a brief touch of his finger to her lips.

Works every time, he thought. His touch made her aware of him as a man, and Helena had reason to be skittish around men. He really shouldn't use that as a weapon. It really wasn't fair, except he liked the feel of her skin beneath his so very much, it was hell not to allow himself these brief seconds of contact now and then.

"No one likes feeling useless, sweetheart," he said. "I'm a man used to keeping busy. You could at least take pity on me and give me something to do."

"Okay," she said, laughing. "I understand the need to be productive." She handed him some vegetables and a cutting board.

"I know you're dying to chop up these green peppers yourself," he said a bit mournfully. "But I truly appreciate you allowing me to help." He wondered if she would ever allow him to help her in any other way. Some more concrete way. This was, after all, what he'd come to Sloane's Cove to do. To help.

But for now he simply studied the lady.

She had donned an austere white apron this time. Very clinical. Very no-nonsense. Only a tiny embroidered strand of pink roses trailing down one strap and hovering near her breast. Damn, but it was driving him insane. He'd never had an urge to even go near an apron, much less remove one from a woman with his teeth, but those very hot thoughts were torturing him right now. That and the fact that Helena had been working her tail off for him ever since he'd arrived. He was going to have to talk to Abe about convincing her to accept a raise. He'd have to be very tactful about it. He had the distinct feeling that Helena was going to consider a deal a deal. She was going to insist they stick to the original terms.

She waited until he'd finished chopping the peppers and tearing up the lettuce for a salad, then handed him a folder.

"More information I've gathered. You want me to show you my treasures, then you have to work a little on your own treasure hunt, Mr. Castle," she coaxed.

"You just don't want me to help you with the cooking," he teased.

"I'm a temperamental chef," she admitted with a shake of her head, which sent her caramel-colored ponytail sliding against the pale skin of her neck.

"You're the least temperamental person I know."

"You say that now, but just keep trying to interfere in my kitchen and you'll see what a tyrant I can be. Now sit, Jackson. Go over your notes. Your tribute to Oliver is only a week and a half away. You've got to choose. Thank goodness it's you and not me making those decisions. You'll need quiet. I'll just be tiptoeing around finishing up lunch. You won't even hear me breathe. Won't even know I'm around," she said.

As if that could ever happen in ten thousand million years, Jackson thought thirty minutes later. He looked up from the papers he'd been perusing and watched her slow sexy smile as she stirred and simmered something over the stove. The soft curve of her cheek made a man want to touch, the look on her face was like that of a lover setting out to please her partner.

"Damn," he said, breaking the pencil he'd been clutching.

"Frustrating?" she asked.

"Incredibly," he agreed.

"I've got just the thing," she promised, and he almost groaned.

Moving closer, close enough that he could breathe in the lemon scent of her and feel the warmth of her skin, she held out a spoon in an enticing fashion.

"Here, taste," she offered. "All for you."

"What is it?" he asked.

"Paradise on a spoon. Just taste."

He leaned forward. She slipped the spoon between his teeth.

The moan of pleasure that escaped his lips earned him a satisfied chuckle.

"What is it?" he asked again. "Besides paradise."

She shrugged. "Something I just made up. I thought that it would do for the party you're going to have when you gather all your candidates together to make your final decision."

"Looks like it's going to be a big party," he said, gesturing to his piles of notes. "You know a lot about a lot of people."

Helena frowned slightly. "I know. It seems... wrong somehow to talk about such personal matters, or at least to put it all down on paper. If I didn't think it was for a good cause, I wouldn't be doing this."

Jackson felt a twinge of conscience himself. Not at seeking out the details of people's lives, because he knew he'd never use that information for anything wrong, but because he was distressing Helena with what he'd asked her to do.

"I hadn't thought how difficult this would be for you," he began. "Helena, you don't have to do this anymore. I've got enough information. There's no need for you to have to—"

She shook her head suddenly, and the small band that was holding her hair back while she cooked slid away, freeing the long strands of silk. "No, that's not it. I love what you're doing. I'm glad to be able to help. Not just you, but everyone. How many people ever have this kind of opportunity to really make a difference? It's just that—I don't know. I've never analyzed my friendships so much. I've never delved beneath the surface of people's existences so deeply. Most of the time things just are. They just happen without thought, don't they?"

They certainly did, Jackson thought, crossing his arms to keep himself from gathering her into his embrace, to keep himself from kissing her, from just letting things happen without thought. He'd married without thought or feeling or the ability to give and be what a husband should be. He wasn't going to make that mistake again, wasn't going to live that hell again.

He'd grown up knowing he didn't have the ability

to give as other men did, to feel as they did. The valve that controlled those finer emotions had been shut off. So he wasn't going to make the mistake of moving forward without thought again.

"You're a good friend, Helena," he said softly. "A good neighbor. And a cook without rival. Let's taste some more of that paradise you've created, and then you'll show me your work, the things you do after dark."

She almost never let anyone into her office, into her sanctuary, Helena realized as she pushed open the door and revealed her most private space to Jackson.

"I would have cleaned this place up if I'd known I was going to have company," she said, bunching her shoulders in embarrassment.

She started to move forward to straighten the sliding mass of papers on her desk and Jackson stilled her with a brief touch of his hand.

"Someday I'll take you to Boston and show you my own office," he promised. "My secretary threatens to call the fire marshal every time she has to step into the room."

A small laugh escaped Helena's lips. "Okay, I'm not going to try to one-up you on that one. You're sure you want to see this stuff?"

"I don't make claims I don't mean."

His voice was low and strong and committed. Helena was sure he was a man who went through with what he started. He didn't make promises if he didn't intend to keep them. She was pretty sure he didn't make very many promises at all.

"Here's my collection," she said, opening the glass doors of an oak bookshelf. "Such as it is."

Jackson gave a low whistle. "You've been writing for a long time."

She shrugged one shoulder, feeling as if she were standing naked before a man for the first time, flaws and all. "They haven't all been sold, you understand. Some of them I've had printed up for my own use or for community fund-raisers. But yes, my father said that I was born with a spoon and a pan in my hands. My mother died when I was ten and I took over all the family's cooking. I haven't stopped since."

Jackson ran one hand over the shiny spines of the books. "May I look inside?" he asked, reaching out.

"Of course. They're made to be read."

But her breath caught with nervousness as he reverently turned back the pages of her latest creation. For long moments silence filled the room, broken only by the soft rustle of paper against paper. Then Jackson looked up from the book he was holding. "This is incredible," he said, his voice filled with admiration. "Helena, these are more than mere collections of recipes, even though I'm certain the recipes themselves would be treasure enough. You've included bits of trivia about the backgrounds of the dishes, local folklore. I'm guessing this border work was done by Ward Sheridan. I've seen his stuff in town."

"He's a master, isn't he?" she asked.

Jackson leveled his silvery glance on her. "He's not the only one. These are more than cookbooks, Helena," he said, picking up another volume and flipping through. "This one has a poem that goes with every recipe. These are books a person would settle down with and read just for the pleasure of reading. You've put more than just your mouthwatering recipes inside these covers. You've brought yourself right into the reader's kitchen. That's pretty special."

He glanced down at her, and Helena hoped that tears weren't welling up in her eyes. She feared they were. These books were just cookbooks to most people. Just road maps to making a good meal, but to her, well, her heart was poured into them. This was where she went when something good happened to her—or something bad. This was what she'd done when she was getting over her losses and celebrating her successes. No one had ever found her out until now. It was a relief to have someone discover her deepest secret.

"Thank you," she said quietly.

He laughed lightly, helping her get past the awkwardness of the emotional moment. "For what, Helena? For having eyes to see? What man wouldn't?"

She couldn't answer that one. She simply stared up at him.

It seemed the most natural thing in the world that while he was staring down at her, she should lean closer, he should cover the distance. It was no surprise at all that he tilted his head and covered her lips with his own.

It was only what came afterward that surprised her. Longing, sharp and deep, ripped through her.

"Helena," Jackson said, pulling back a bit. And then his lips met hers again.

She pressed herself close, snaked her arms around his neck. His kiss was dark and hungry, flavorful and demanding.

"Closer. Now," he demanded when she came up for air.

And she was swept up, moved forward into his

dizzying embrace. She felt as if her body had no borders, no limits, that she flowed straight into Jackson's body and became a part of him.

Except she wanted more. The ache that was growing inside her was demanding and edgy.

She tore her lips from his and kissed his throat.

He lifted her against him and teased her apron and blouse away with his mouth. His lips caressed the skin above her collarbone. And then the skin below.

His hair was dark silk sliding through her fingers, his touch a torment that made her long to move closer, remove any barriers between them.

Jackson dropped to his knees before her. He twined his arms around her thighs. He kissed her at that most sensitive juncture of her body, his breath warm and moist through the thin cloth that separated his lips from her body.

A groan ripped through him.

A gasp escaped Helena.

And then the baby kicked. Hard.

Helena jerked.

Jackson froze. For a second his eyes looked shocked. Something akin to pain seeped into his expression. He stared at her abdomen as if he had forgotten she was carrying a child, as if he had committed a crime beyond redemption. Finally he leaned back on his heels and gazed up at her, though he didn't release her, not completely.

Slowly, gracefully, he loosened his grip, rose to his feet and stepped away from her.

"I forgot myself, but, well, I doubt it's any secret that I've been wanting to touch you for days," he said, his voice low and gentle. "Still, I think we'd both agree that this wasn't exactly wise."

She knew it was the complete opposite of everything that was wise. Now she knew how deeply she could want him.

"No," she agreed softly. "I suppose we'd be crazy to ever do it again."

"We won't," he promised. "You have things you need to be thinking of right now. Making love with a man who's leaving in a week and a half probably isn't one of them."

She couldn't answer that. She didn't want to allow herself the total vision of what it would be like to truly make love with Jackson—or to watch him leave.

Helena shook her head. "You're right. Let me show you the rest of my work."

"Good idea."

But the first book Jackson's hand fell on was the one book she should have warned him away from if she'd only been thinking straight.

"Aphrodisiacs for the Common Man?" he asked, arching his brows. Helena felt herself growing pink and warm.

She reached for the book.

He stepped away. "I'm looking."

"Give it back."

"Other people have seen it. It's published, and I haven't even opened it yet."

"Stubborn man."

"You bet. Come on. I want to see this. This promises to be really good stuff and very important, too. Ask any man."

And Helena realized that this light touch was just what she and Jackson needed.

"I'm very proud of that book," she said, trying to

look down her nose at a man who was taller than she was.

"Be proud, Helena," he urged. "You should be." His hand hovered over the volume. "Mind if I...borrow this?"

His totally unexpected question was enough to jolt her out of her embarrassment at her flare of passion and lack of restraint. "What do you want with it?"

His lips curved into the slightest of smiles and her heart shivered. "This is a side of you I haven't seen. I'd just like to see what personal touches you've added to this book."

She wrinkled her nose, but she didn't argue with him borrowing the book. "I'll have you know that it's very clinical," she said, trying not to smile but not succeeding.

He laughed. "Lady, there's absolutely nothing clinical about you."

He held the door for her as they exited the room and made their way out her front door. The book on aphrodisiacs was in his hand, its gold lettering clearly visible to anyone watching them.

She'd always been proud of that book. It had taken a lot of research and hard work to produce. But she couldn't help wondering what her brothers would think if they heard that it was now in Jackson's possession.

Chapter Seven

She was going to have to stay away from Jackson's lips, Helena thought the next morning as she pushed the vacuum cleaner over the floor.

That embrace had left her trembling for hours. Moreover, the moment when Jackson had felt her baby kick was probably going to be emblazoned on her memory forever. That startled, guarded look followed by regret. He had forgotten for a moment that she was pregnant, but once he'd remembered, he'd quickly backed away.

"And why not?" she muttered. "The man made it very clear from the start he wasn't interested in commitment. You can't fault him for that."

At least he'd been decent enough to let her know how things stood. No other man had ever been that honest before.

So why was she feeling so sad this morning?

Because I'm pregnant, of course. Emotional. And because for a moment there she'd felt beautiful, not big. And gosh darn it, because Jackson Castle was the first man ever who had looked at her work and made her feel that it was really special, that he understood.

That didn't mean she wanted to let anything mess with the safe life's plan she'd made. All she needed was baby Austin-to-be and her work.

She wrestled the vacuum cleaner deeper into a corner.

"I'm not letting myself be a bull's-eye for heartache again," she said vehemently. "And Jackson Castle is dead certain heartache. No question, that man has kissed thousands of women. He's slain hundreds of hearts. And none of them were humongously pregnant. Except for his wife."

His wife. Helena wondered what the woman had looked like. She wondered if her sister, Lilah, had any old back issues of magazines that would have shown the woman.

And that was it. Helena stopped in her tracks. She stood there leaning on the vacuum cleaner counting the seconds until sanity returned. She couldn't believe she was actually torturing herself with worries about how lovely Jackson's ex-wife or any of his other women had been.

Not when, in a matter of days, she would just be an ex-cook, just another woman Jackson had once kissed in a brief mad moment and then walked away from.

She'd been walked away from too many times.

So, leave.

"I can't," she whispered loudly.

The reasons were complex. They went beyond the fact that she wanted the chance to try her skills on those who would come to Jackson's gathering, or that she wanted to help her friends.

The fact was that, rich as he was, Jackson had old scars from people walking away from him, too. His mother. His wife. And in spite of the fact that he was uncomfortable letting people get too close, he was here trying to do a good thing. How could she ignore those things?

So stay. Deal with the risk.

Helena gave the vacuum a long hard push as if to punctuate her thoughts, and shut off the machine. She blew out a breath that raised the bangs on her forehead. She hugged her arms close to her.

"Helena?"

Jackson's deep voice was filled with dread.

She turned to look at him filling up the doorway. He was staring at the vacuum cleaner as if it had grown three heads and was spitting fire.

"They ought to put warnings on those things. You're hurt, aren't you?"

Was she? Was that why her lips felt suddenly tight and bruised, as if they'd feel better only if he'd kiss her again?

"I'm not hurt," she said with a gentle shake of her head. "I'm just—I don't know. A vacuum cleaner is kind of like this big beast you get to push around that eats dirt. I'm just savoring my victory over dust mites everywhere," she said, trying to smile and shove her wayward thoughts aside. If she kept things light, she'd be just fine.

"A big beast?"

"Ferocious?"

"Heavy," he stated, eyeing the thing again.

"Don't do that," she told him.

"Do what?" He crossed his arms, crossed his ankles and gazed at her, a lazy smile lifting his lips.

"You're taking charge again. Planning something. Is this how you manhandle your clients when they tell you they want gaudy gold sea horses dancing across their bathroom walls and you've already decided that some tasteful miniature prints are what they really need?"

"Ah, you've discovered my secret," he whispered with an arch of his brow.

"You're dreadfully transparent," she told him.

"Am I?"

Helena grabbed the vacuum cleaner handle, desperate for something to hold on to. She had a feeling this was a trick question.

"What am I thinking then, Helena?" he asked, his voice low and sexy.

She raised her chin. She was used to dealing with the haughty rich. Just like him, she was used to offering things at times that her clients hadn't known they wanted.

"You're thinking that we need to go to town to make sure those framed prints of Oliver are finished and ready for display and to see if Mr. Winters has taken care of obtaining a podium and sound system."

Jackson tilted his head. "Clever lady. Actually, I *was* thinking that I need to go into town. Maybe a bit farther than Sloane's Cove, though. Ellsworth or maybe even Bangor. There's something I need to take care of."

"Some business?"

"It could be called business. What does your doctor say about you doing heavy labor?" His gaze was now firmly fixed on the vacuum cleaner again.

She laughed. "He says that digging ditches might not be wise, but anything that's not out of the norm for any other woman is fine for me. I'm healthy, Jackson."

"You're close, aren't you?"

"I won't fail you. I still have three weeks."

"Are you uncomfortable?"

Around him? Always, but only because she was so aware of his maleness.

She shook her head. "I could vacuum three more houses and not feel tired."

A frown marred his forehead. "You're not going to, are you? I mean, you don't have any side jobs I don't know about? No plans to move furniture around or climb up on ladders to clean windows?"

And then she couldn't hold back her smile. "Would you like me to have Dr. Vargas give you a call to ascertain that I am, in fact, completely capable of going on with my life? I'll be fine, Jackson. I won't fail you."

"You've probably never failed anyone—unless it was yourself."

"I'm not a martyr, Jackson. I don't risk my child's life or health."

He nodded. He went away, seemingly satisfied at last.

Hours later when he returned, Helena understood why. She came out of the kitchen, untying the strings on her apron. John Nesbith was wheeling a riding vacuum cleaner into the living room.

"Hey, Helena, look what Jackson bought. Isn't it great?"

"It's...astounding," she said, covering her mouth with one hand. Oh my, just what had the man gone and done? And why? She was going to be working here only another week and a half. What was he going to do with this thing then?

"He took me with him," John was saying excitedly. "Look, Jackson made sure he got one with a tilt steering wheel so you wouldn't be—you know, smushed where your baby is. And he made sure it wouldn't go too fast and that it had every safety feature they could put on one of these things. I've never seen anyone fire so many questions at a salesman before. Jackson surely knows how to get what he wants."

But as Jackson came through the doorway, studying her with those dark demanding eyes, Helena couldn't help wondering, what did he really want?

Later that night she lay in bed trying not to dwell on thoughts of Jackson. "I think what he really wants is a job well done. To keep me healthy so that we can finish up here before the baby comes. To leave as soon as his mission is over."

And what did she want?

She wanted things to be over now before she got in any deeper than she was. But she also wanted something else. She wanted to make sure that Jackson knew that his wife had been wrong. There was no way anyone could ever think of him as a cold, unfeeling man.

He had deep feelings. He just hid them inside, thinking that they belonged to himself alone. But they were so very clear if one only paid attention.

What kind of man went out of his way to provide a pregnant employee with a riding vacuum cleaner he would never use again?

"A kind man," she whispered as her eyes drifted

shut. "A generous man. A man you'd better not dream about tonight."

She slid into sleep and dreamed of Jackson, but at least part of that dreaming was constructive. By morning she had not discovered a way to show him that his wife had been wrong, but she had at least decided on a small way she could help repay him for his kindness.

"What is this secret mission we're on, Helena?" Jackson asked the next afternoon. "Something to do with the tribute to Oliver?"

She shook her head and smiled as she steered the car around a turn. "Sort of, but not really. Thank you for letting me drive."

"Your doctor told me that you were allowed to."

Her head swung around. "You called him?"

Was that pale pink singeing Jackson's jawline? Surely not.

"More like I...bumped into him in town. Purposely."

Yes, that was definitely a touch of pink.

"I'll admit that it was a bit out of line, but I just wanted to make sure that I wasn't asking too much of you."

"And now you know that you aren't."

"Apparently so. The good doctor told me that you were happiest keeping busy and taking care of people and that it was important that you remain happy. I suspect that was a warning to me not to cause you any distress. Your brothers aren't the only ones worrying about you."

"It's part of the small-town thing," she conceded with a slight shrug.

"I suspect it's more that you just tend to inspire those kinds of protective feelings in people."

He was wrong about that. There'd been plenty of people who hadn't felt that way about her, but that wasn't a topic she wanted to go into right now.

"Here we are," she said quietly, pulling into a drive.

Jackson turned and looked at the view straight ahead. A modest white cottage was set back off a small boulder-strewn beach.

"This looks...familiar," Jackson said. "Vaguely familiar."

"I'd hoped that it would. I sent out a few feelers. One of my friends is a member of the historical society and he has collections of some of the guest books from the rental properties. It seems that once upon a time, a man named Oliver Davis stayed here for a few weeks several summers. I think this must have been the place where you met him."

Jackson's laugh was low and rich. "Not really. I met Oliver in the center of a crowd coming back from a fireworks exhibition on the Fourth of July. That was where I tried to pick his pockets. But he did bring me here once. It was where he negotiated with my mother to help oversee my care and education."

Something in the way he said "negotiated" made Helena's blood turn chilly. What kind of a mother would "negotiate" her child out of her home?

"Perhaps we shouldn't have come here," she said hesitantly.

Long strong fingers tucked beneath her chin, turned her to face him. "I dealt away the past years ago, Helena. My mother gave up on me before I was ever even born. So the only emotion this place evokes in me is gratitude that I was lucky enough to be in the right place at the right time and that Oliver was good enough to help me.''

She tried to believe that he was telling the truth, but she knew that she should have been less impulsive and asked him if he'd wanted to come here before she just forged ahead.

"It's all right, Helena," he said, as if her thoughts were written in her eyes. "I'm glad we've come. This was, after all, the place where my life changed for the better."

"Would you like to go inside? The owner's visiting the national park today. He said it was all right."

Jackson studied Helena's worried expression and knew that no force on earth could have made him divulge the truth, that he felt his chest closing up at the prospect of going inside. Helena had brought him here because she'd cared. He would darn well make sure she knew he appreciated it. And in a sense, he *was* glad they'd come.

As they walked through the place that had once been elegant but had grown shabby with time, he admitted that he'd needed this.

"Is it at all the same?" Helena asked softly.

"Some. The leaded-glass windows are cracked but they're still solid. The fireplace is just as I remember it, even if the wood on the mantel is a bit scarred. The furnishings are mostly different. The sofa used to be cobalt blue. Oliver loved bright things." He also loved promising individuals, Jackson remembered. He'd questioned whether he had the right to ask Jackson's mother to allow him to send him away to school.

But he needn't have worried. Jackson's mother had been overjoyed to get rid of her responsibility.

He'd never seen her after that day. She'd never even tried to reconnect, but his twelve years with her had marked him. Every woman who'd ever told him he was too distant, that he was incapable of giving and receiving love, reminded him of that, that some things never changed. So did this house.

But the house also reminded him that he was a very lucky man. He'd been given a chance to escape and to do the kinds of things he excelled at. If forging lasting relationships wasn't one of those things, so be it. It was always good to be reminded of one's weaknesses and strengths. Oliver had helped him discover his strengths, had shown him that he had some.

Jackson took a deep breath and called up a vision of a man with kind, worried eyes, a man who had believed in saving children one by one whenever he could. He'd done a good job, Jackson thought. He'd made a difference in a few lives, which was more than most men did. He'd cared enough to reach out where there was a need.

Stepping to the mantelpiece, Jackson picked up a shell.

"Oliver loved seashells," he said. "I'd almost forgotten that. I met him once in Florida and we just walked along the beach picking up shells. He was a grown man who was almost innocent in many ways, especially in his enthusiasm about helping others. I hope that those of us who benefited from his kindness gave at least a little something back to him. I have the feeling that most of us were too caught up in making sure our pasts didn't come back to haunt us to relax enough to even say thank-you. I won't make that mistake again, Helena. Thank you for bringing me here. It was an experience I needed."

She moved closer. She touched the shell he was still holding. She looked up into his eyes.

"You don't look happy," she said, her voice soft and questioning.

He shook off the memories that assailed him, the thought that there were things a man could change and things he could never change. He forced a smile.

"I'm not completely happy," he teased, surprising a startled look into those deep blue eyes.

"That is, I'd be a lot happier if I weren't hungry," he whispered, knowing exactly where her weaknesses lay and aiming straight at the target. "I didn't know that dredging up the past could make a man so ravenous."

Bingo. She smiled up at him. "Well, then, if you're hungry, that's a problem I can fix," she said. "I happen to be a very good cook. I can make anything you like."

"Even love potions," he reminded her.

She wrinkled her nose. "Aphrodisiacs are not love potions. Their purpose is to stimulate the…"

He grinned more broadly when she hesitated.

"Forget that. Let's go get something to eat," she said, looking toward the door.

"Maybe coco-de-mer," he added, naming something he'd found in her aphrodisiac book.

"Maybe a fresh fruit salad and a hearty vegetable soup," she said, sounding very prim.

"Umm, I love it when you talk food," he said with a smile.

"Are you trying to make me forget what you told me about your mother back there?"

He tucked one finger under her chin and leaned closer. "I'm trying to tell you that I appreciate you. You did a nice thing. I'm grateful and I'm happy, Helena. I'm very happy. You don't have to worry."

If there was going to be worrying done—about why he couldn't seem to keep this woman off his mind when he knew darn well that he had no future with her—then *he* would be the one to do the worrying.

The sun was sinking in the sky that same day when Jackson finished with his phone call from Boston. It was a good thing his work here would be done soon. There were details of his business that needed seeing to and not everything could be done long-distance.

The words *long distance* made him wonder where Helena was. He'd had to insist that she take breaks more often. She tended to forget if he didn't nag her. She'd finally agreed to get some fresh air, but she hadn't returned yet, and that wasn't like Helena.

A sense of unease drifted through him. He stepped out onto the deck and looked down toward the sea path. About one hundred yards from the base of his steps he saw her, standing on the wide ocean path, her telltale long hair billowing out around her, her shoes dangling from one hand.

He saw something else, too. She wasn't alone. There was a man walking toward her. A familiar-looking man, and it wasn't one of the Austin brothers. From this elevation he could see clearly, but Helena and Barrett would have to look up to see him. It was obvious from Barrett's confident stride that he thought they were alone.

Jackson's sense of unease grew.

"It's my responsibility to make sure nothing happens to her,'' he muttered. That was, of course, the only reason he was alarmed, he assured himself as he started down the steps. At the base of the steps scrubby pines lined the winding trail that led to the ocean path. They blocked his view of Helena, but the air was still along the coast at this hour. Sound traveled clearly over the short distance that separated them.

''I've missed seeing you, Helena,'' Barrett was saying.

''I'm surprised to hear that. We don't really know each other, do we?''

''A man doesn't need to know a woman to see that she's beautiful. I've spent too much of my time these last few days on business. When I saw you on the path, I knew this was my lucky day. Looking at you is a pleasure.''

''Thank you.''

''I'd like to see more of you.''

Jackson almost stopped dead in his tracks as anger overtook him. Instead he rounded a switchback that brought him lower and closer, but still not close enough to see clearly.

''Why?'' she asked. ''Why do you want to see more of me?''

''I'd think that was obvious, Helena. I've already told you that you're beautiful. What more need a man say before taking the next step?'' Barrett's voice had turned deep and suggestive. As the trail that led from Jackson's house took a final turn and intercepted a wider path, Jackson glanced to his left. Barrett was looking down at Helena as if he'd like to devour her.

Jackson was feeling as if he'd like to feed Barrett to the fish. For a moment he couldn't even move as he struggled to regain control of his emotions. He was pretty sure that Barrett's suddenly rigid stance meant that he'd noticed he had company. But Helena's back was to Jackson. He couldn't see her face to see her reaction to Barrett's suggestion.

"Are you trying to flirt with me, Mr. Richards?" she asked.

Barrett chuckled. "Finally we're making progress. I am most definitely trying to flirt with you, Helena. Do you mind?"

Jackson minded.

"I'm...not sure," Helena answered. "As I said, I don't really know you."

"Then allow me to get to know you," Barrett said, his brow arching in a dare as he looked up at Jackson. "I've heard plenty of things about you since I've come here. All kinds of tales circulating about your culinary skill, the way you're the queen of good causes. Fascinating stuff. I'd really like to have the opportunity to know more." He took a slight step nearer to her.

Cold, icy anger hardened Jackson's jaw and he quickly moved closer, stones crunching beneath his feet. He nodded to Helena as she turned at his approach, but his true target was the man standing much too close to her. He struggled to control his impulse to return to his old ways of using his fists rather than his words.

"Hello, Barrett," Jackson said quietly.

"What a surprise to see you, Jackson. I assumed Ms. Austin was on her own time. Guess you've been keeping her busier than I thought." The man's smile was practiced and knowing.

Jackson refused to justify his time with Helena. He

simply looked at her, trying to read her feelings. Did she want him to stay or to leave? But he couldn't just leave when she didn't know what she was up against here. He'd heard Barrett's speech. He knew from experience that the man could be charming and convincing.

"It's a busy summer" was all that he said. "Are you tired, Helena?"

He turned his full attention to her. She was smiling at him.

"I *am* feeling a bit tired, Jackson," she admitted. "I guess I walked farther than I'd realized. Are you ready to go now?"

More than ready. He was dying to get her away from there. He wanted to hold out his hand, but he didn't want to give Barrett anything to latch on to, any reason to target her more than he already was. "Let's go...back," he said. He'd meant to say, "Let's go home," but that, too, wouldn't have escaped Barrett's attention.

The lady confounded all his good intentions by stepping up to him and placing her hand on his arm. "I'm ready," she said willingly. "Goodbye, Mr. Richards."

Barrett's laugh was sly. "Got there first again, did you, Jackson?"

Jackson turned his expression icy and haughty. He knew how to do that when he had to. "Don't say anything ugly, Barrett. You *will* regret it. I'll personally see to that."

Barrett's brows drew together in a long, thick line. Just as quickly, he masked his reaction with a short burst of laughter. "Perhaps that's a dare I'll take you up on. At any rate, I'll see you around, Jackson, I'm sure. Goodbye, Helena. For now.''

Jackson didn't speak until they were back at the house. Helena didn't argue when he pulled out a chair and indicated that she should sit, even though she usually argued that she was perfectly capable of taking care of herself.

Still, she'd been silent several minutes while he was sitting there trying to decide how best to approach the subject of Barrett.

"Something's wrong, isn't it?" she finally asked, touching her hand to his knee. "You dislike him even more than I'd realized."

He turned his head to the side, unable to look at her when he spoke.

"He can be quite charming."

"I suppose he can," she said, confusion lacing her voice.

"You might be thinking he's a man you would like to get to know better. Women consider him handsome, I've been told."

"That wouldn't surprise me."

Jackson swung back around, a lock of dark hair falling forward. "I'm going to sound like a jerk asking you this. I have no right to ask anything this personal, but…are you considering spending any more time with Barrett?"

Her chin rose just slightly. He knew he'd overstepped a boundary. "I grew up with four brothers who wanted to live my life and failed. I've made mistakes, but at least they've been my own. I've allowed you to fuss because I know my…condition bothers you, but…there's nothing between you and me, Jackson. There's no reason for me to enter into this war you and Barrett are waging.''

Jackson listened to the words. "I agree with you on principle. You're right, and I shouldn't interfere, but I can't just say nothing. He's married," he said carefully.

Helena's eyes opened wide.

"I wasn't implying anything about you," he began.

She shook her head. "I didn't think you were. You were worried about me, but there's no need. I hope I don't sound naive, but I never would have guessed the man was married. My husband fell in love with another woman after we were married, but he didn't openly flirt with her on the streets.''

Her husband. The father of the baby she was carrying.

His concern must have shown in his eyes.

"I told you before, Jackson, Peter and I weren't in love," she insisted. "And I'm not in any danger from Barrett, either. Not now, and not ten minutes ago before I knew the truth. As I've told you before, I'm not looking for love. I'm not susceptible. You won't have to worry. There's no chance that Barrett Richards can have his way with me.''

And maybe no other man could, or should, have his way with her, either, Jackson thought. But the woman's eyes, soft body and warm heart could still keep a man restless, without sleep and groaning for hours as he conjured up forbidden fantasies....

Chapter Eight

The first sight that greeted Jackson after he woke up two mornings later was Helena seated in the kitchen talking to a man. An incredibly handsome, smiling man.

The man stood up when Jackson walked into the room. He held out his hand.

"Good morning, Mr. Castle. I'm Eric Ryan, a friend of Helena's brothers. A friend of Helena's, too, of course."

Another suitor. Of course.

Jackson hazarded a glance Helena's way, but the lady wasn't wearing that harassed look she usually wore when these men came to call. On the contrary, she was smiling brightly. She wanted this man here.

And he'd promised himself after that episode with Barrett that he wouldn't interfere in her life anymore.

"It's a pleasure meeting you, Jackson," Eric was saying. "You've certainly added some excitement to all of our lives lately. I've given more tours this week than I usually give the entire month of June.''

''Eric works for one of the whale-watching expeditions, but he also builds boats,'' Helena said with pride.

''More like, I try to build boats when I have the time.''

''Someday you'll be known up and down the coast,'' she predicted.

At the warmth in her voice, Jackson felt something snarling and painful start to grow inside him. He fought to subdue the beast. He concentrated on the man before him.

''I'd like to see your work someday,'' Jackson offered. ''I have an interest in such things.'' Not to mention that he had an interest in making sure that this man was as wholesome as he appeared. Helena might say that she wanted no man, but she was clearly enamored of this one.

''I think you'll be impressed,'' Helena said. ''Eric's an artist when he gets to work. Believe me, I know. When we were kids, my brothers and Lilah and I used to build makeshift houses out of whatever we could find lying around. Eric's structures always put the rest of us to shame.''

''You never said so then. You were the one who always declared herself the winner when we had a contest,'' Eric said with a laugh.

''Hey, I couldn't let a mere male best me, now, could I? Still, you show Jackson what you do. He'll want to see. I have this teeny tendency to be biased, he's discovered.''

And to show her feelings in her eyes, Jackson thought, watching her glow for Eric Ryan.

"I'm biased where my oldest, closest friends are concerned, too," Eric said as he started to rise. "But I'd better go now. Work to do. Thank you for the coffee," he said to both Helena and Jackson.

Jackson nodded, still studying the man. "Nice to have met you, Eric. And I meant that about your business. I'm always interested in new talent."

The man tilted his head a bit sheepishly. "Will do, but don't feel any need to do this just because I'm Helena's friend. I didn't come for that."

Jackson knew full well why the man had come.

"I don't make business deals unless I'm impressed with the work," he agreed. "And I know you didn't come to discuss your boats."

A slight flush broke over the man's skin. He turned to Helena.

"About the other thing, I—"

"Don't worry about it," she said.

"Still friends?"

"Always friends," she agreed, taking his hand. "That will never change."

The man's smile rivaled the morning sunlight and he winked at Helena just before he said his goodbyes.

Silence filled the kitchen. The clock ticked loudly on the wall. Jackson thought he could hear the house breathing.

"He came to solicit your hand in marriage," he said slowly.

"We're old friends."

"Marrying old friends?"

She shook her head vehemently. "Of course not. I told you that wasn't what I wanted."

He knew that, but he'd also seen what was in her eyes. And this man, this Eric, seemed to be a good man. Maybe a very good man. The kind of man she deserved. The kind of man who would always be here for her.

"You might change your mind. You might be interested later."

Helena gave an exasperated shake of her head. "What I'm interested in now is Eric being able to follow his dream. For years he's poured most of his money into taking care of his aging parents. He's never had a chance to do what he wants to do, but he really is incredibly talented, Jackson. If you think his work has value, he might be one of the three."

And for the first time, Jackson realized that he really might be biased, after all. This man made him burn and seethe inside, but he knew that was pure jealousy. This man might belong to Helena someday. In spite of what she'd said, she might change her mind once the baby was here. He wanted to help *her,* but she didn't need his help in any tangible way. Not his money, not anything he could give her. But he could help the man she might someday love.

"I'll look at his work," he promised. "Maybe we can add a fourth beneficiary."

Helena blinked at his words. Jackson had a calculating look in those beautiful silvery eyes of his. He was looking at her as if she'd grown more fragile.

"You're doing this for me."

"I respect your judgment."

"You also have a thing about helping women," she said suddenly. "You're beginning to remind me a bit of my brothers."

"That's not the worst thing in the world."

"You wouldn't say that if you'd known that

Thomas called me yesterday to ask why you were
seen carrying my aphrodisiac book out of my house.''

"Ah, so he called you, too. What did you tell
him?"

"I told him you and I were having wild orgies,"
she lied. "What did you tell him?"

"I told him that you were tying me to the bed and
force-feeding me your wicked potions.''

"You always know just the right thing to say to
my brothers," she teased.

"And you always seem to have a way of getting
me off the subject." Half a lazy smile formed on
Jackson's lips. "You're not implying that you don't
want me to help your friend?''

"No, I—"

She just didn't want him to do it because he felt
obligated—because of her. She knew he'd felt guilty
that he'd let Barrett get her alone. She'd seen the way
his breath had caught in his throat when she'd mentioned that her husband had been in love with another
woman. She already knew that he felt guilty about the
way things had gone with his wife.

"You don't owe me anything, Jackson. Any mistakes I made in my life I made on my own. Any
things I chose to do, including working for you, I
chose on my own. You can't change my past by doing
me favors.''

"I'm not trying to change the past. Not any of it.''

And an idea began to form in her mind. "Your
wife—''

He smiled and shook his head slightly. "No, don't
start down that path, Helena. My ex-wife has nothing
to do with this," he said, his voice soothing. "I'm
not repeating history, trying to make amends with you

as the surrogate woman. Denise was nothing like you, and it was a simple story. I married her because she was this pretty, cheerful little thing, almost like another work of art I'd picked up. I cheated her out of the affection she needed.''

"So she went looking for it elsewhere. That was wrong, Jackson. At least while she was still married to you.''

Then the tumblers—finally—clicked in her mind. ''Barrett—''

He simply nodded. "Barrett, believe it or not, can be very convincing when he wants to. And she wanted a child. I knew that. I didn't even try to understand her needs. Instead, Barrett gave her what she wanted, even if I didn't know at first that the baby was his.''

His voice grew almost imperceptibly rough.

She wondered what he must have felt like, thinking he was going to be a father and then learning that the child was another man's.

"Understand me, Helena," Jackson said, tearing her thoughts from the path they'd gone down. "Another man gave my wife what she needed because I didn't even see that the need was there. I'm not a deeply emotional man. What you get from me, you get because I've looked at all the possibilities and made a rational decision. You understand that?''

She nodded, knowing she lied. She understood nothing except that Jackson believed that he had nothing to give a woman, that he lived with guilt over having cheated his wife of what she needed, that he was acting as her own husband had. Peter had given her a baby because he'd felt guilty about loving another woman.

"I understand," she said, but she couldn't stop her voice from breaking just a bit.

And then Jackson groaned. He dragged her up against him. He plunged his fingers into her hair and slanted his mouth over her own.

Helena opened her mouth and her heart and her soul. This kiss might be the product of guilt and remorse on Jackson's part, but it was all she could have of him.

And she would have him. This day, anyway.

She wrapped her arms around his neck. She clung as the kiss deepened and her senses expanded. Jackson's hands slid to her back, down to her hips, up to cover her breasts.

He groaned into her mouth and pulled her closer, as close as he possibly could.

She breathed in the scent of him, soap and aftershave and toothpaste and man. Her lips softened beneath his. She slid her hand over his newly shaved jaw. She murmured against his mouth.

And she heard the distant tapping of knuckles on glass.

"Damn." Jackson's oath was muffled against her mouth as he pulled back and gently, hastily made sure her clothing wasn't unbuttoned.

Together they looked up and saw Alma peering through the window.

Helena closed her eyes and moaned. "Prepare yourself for the fallout."

"Alma likes to talk, does she?" Jackson whispered with a slight chuckle in his voice.

"You've noticed that, have you? What do you think this will mean?"

"A shotgun in my back once your brothers hear of it?"

"Don't worry. I'll protect you," she said, patting his cheek and mocking the words he'd said on one of his first days here.

"Like hell you will, Helena," he muttered.

She laughed as they went to let Alma in, and she realized she felt giddy. The passionate moment had been broken, but for the first time in days, she and Jackson were keeping things light.

It was the smartest thing they could do, she was sure.

Put this kiss behind them and go on as they had started. Soon enough they'd be saying goodbye, and she wanted no regrets or haunting memories.

Jackson stared down at the bit of cloth he held in his hands. For several seconds he felt foolishly ridiculous for having bought the thing. He hadn't minded at all when Alma had caught him kissing Helena yesterday, but this was different. This was not the kind of gift a man gave a woman. He couldn't imagine what had possessed him when he'd passed the tiny shop in Bar Harbor.

But he did know. Helena had a weakness for aprons. He had a weakness for Helena in her aprons.

And this one reminded him of her. Made of a white the color of the clouds in the harbor, it had a cut-lace scalloped edging and a white-on-white rose appliquéd around the band of the bib. Made of material so fine it was somewhat fragile and would probably be of no practical use at all, it was a silly gift.

He gave it to her as soon as he stepped inside the door.

"Jackson, it's lovely. Thank you so much. Here, put it on me," she whispered, reaching behind her to untie the blue cotton ties of the sensible apron she'd donned that morning.

Jackson pulled the apron from her shoulders, drew it forward over her breasts and freed her. He had slipped the new one on and was smoothing the material over her—savoring the heady forbidden sensation of touching her—and reaching for the ties when a rapping was heard on the door.

He leaned his lips against the crown of her head, breathed in the soft floral scent of her hair.

"We're making a habit of this lately, aren't we? Getting caught in a damning position."

She turned in his arms and frowned. "You were just tying my apron."

Jackson couldn't help smiling. "Was that all I was doing? Be sure and mention that to Hank, will you?" he teased as Hank opened the door without waiting and stepped into the room. Bill, Thomas and Frank were right behind him, followed by Lilah.

"Don't any of you ever have to work?" Helena asked.

"Still early, sweetie," Bill said. "Most of us don't start work at the crack of dawn the way you do. We've got time to visit."

Helena raised one brow. "And you like visiting at this early hour, do you, Bill? I seem to remember jumping on your stomach to wake you up at ten when we were kids."

Lilah grinned and poked her oldest brother in the ribs with her elbow. "She's got you there, Bill. Don't mind me, Helena," she said. "I'm not here to visit.

I'm just tagging along for moral support. For you, of course. A twin has to stick by her own."

Frank gave Lilah a just-stop-right-there look as he stepped forward, moving straight up into Jackson's face. "We don't exactly need an excuse, Helena, not after we heard that Jackson was kissing you in this very kitchen yesterday."

"He was?" Helena asked, widening her eyes.

Thomas rolled his eyes. "Alma told us it was more than a kiss."

"She wasn't trying to get you in trouble, hon," Lilah said quickly. "It was more like—well, you know Alma. She was excited."

Helena smiled. "I know Alma. I've been expecting all of you."

"So what do you have to say?" Hank demanded. "You know this man's reputation."

"I know a lot more than that," Helena began hotly, and Jackson knew she was going to start defending him. Helena could no more allow someone to be maligned in her presence than she could stop writing recipes.

Gently he placed his hands on her arms and stepped slightly in front of her.

"If you have complaints about the way I'm treating your sister, then I think those complaints should come directly to me."

"I couldn't agree with you more," Bill said coolly.

"Excuse me," Helena began, tapping Jackson on the shoulder and trying to peer past him, but he blocked her body with his own and kept his attention on her brothers. They were just trying to protect her interests after all, and they were right.

"I kissed your sister yesterday," he conceded,

"and I'm not a bit sorry that I did. Helena is a very lovely woman, both inside and out. I'm incredibly attracted to her. Astoundingly so, I might add."

He felt Helena squirm where her hand still rested on him.

"Are you saying you're interested in my sister?" Frank asked.

"If you mean are Helena and I planning to marry, well, I'm afraid that the answer is no, we're not. What I'm saying is that I admire and respect her more than any woman I know or have ever known, both on a personal and a professional level. I'm honored to have had the chance to work with her. I'm delighted to have had the chance just to get to know her. And yes, I'm guilty of sharing a rather heated embrace with your sister. But if you think I'd ever harm her, or allow anyone to harm her in any way, then you're dead wrong. She has nothing to apologize for and she doesn't have to answer to anyone for her actions. I hope I'm being absolutely clear on this issue."

Her brothers were exchanging confused looks, but Helena had obviously had enough of being held in check.

"I love you guys," she said, stepping in front of Jackson and resisting his efforts to shield her, "but honestly, you've gone too far this time. I never in our lifetimes checked up on whom you were kissing or anything else you might have been doing, and I'm sure that you shared more than a peck on the cheek with a whole lot of women before you all got married. What would you have thought if I'd grilled you on every single touch you shared with a woman?"

"This is different," Hank said, crossing his arms.

"Why is it different?"

"You're—well, come on, Helena, you're pregnant. And you're our little sister. We care for you," Thomas said.

"And I care for you, too. But I'm an adult, Thomas. I'm a human being with feelings and the need for privacy and the need to make my own choices. Yes, I am pregnant and soon I'll be a mother," she said, splaying her fingers over her stomach. "I need to be able to make my own decisions as much as possible. You have to let me. No more men coming around here," she added. "You nearly ruined my friendship with Eric, and that has to stop right now."

Frank started to open his mouth. Helena held up her hand. "And Jackson has nothing to apologize for, either. I—I wanted him to kiss me. And if I wanted him to kiss me again, right now, in front of all of you, I'd—well, I'd just say so. And I'd expect you to understand and to stand back and let me do what I wanted."

She was wonderfully magnificent standing there in his kitchen, the kingdom where she ruled. She kept her chin up and absentmindedly pushed back a long strand of hair that had fallen across her cheek as she spoke. She stood there facing her brothers down for his sake and Jackson just couldn't stop himself from leaning forward and whispering in her ear.

"Well, do you, Helena?"

She glanced back over her shoulder. "Do I what?" she asked, her lips just inches away from his own.

"Do you want to kiss me again?" he asked, loud enough for everyone to hear. She wanted her independence. She was standing here demanding it, glorious in her indignation. How could he do anything other than to help her demonstrate that she meant what she said? Especially when she was driving him insane with the need to feel those lips move closer and make contact.

"Do I—want to kiss you again?" she asked softly, her eyes blue and dazed at first. Then she turned and looked up into his eyes. He tried to show her his intent to help her win her independence. She smiled her understanding.

"As a matter of fact, I do want to kiss you again, Jackson," she said. "Very badly." And rising to her toes, she gently looped her arm around his neck.

He lowered his head and tasted her sweetness as she pressed her lips to his. He savored what he knew would be one of his last times to touch Helena.

She drew back. Much too soon. He hadn't nearly had enough of her.

For several seconds she gazed up at him, her eyes dreamy and soft. Then she smiled and turned to her brothers, who were looking like four embarrassed thunderclouds, shuffling their feet against the linoleum.

"Helena?" Thomas asked in a choked voice.

"Oh, leave her alone, Tom," Hank answered. "She's made her point. She's all grown up and just as stubborn as ever."

"See," she said, "that wasn't such a big deal, was it?"

And it was all Jackson could do not to groan. He could swear he heard her brothers chuckling beneath their breath.

Chapter Nine

It was a good thing she had a dinner party to cook for today, Helena thought. Otherwise she'd be spending all her time remembering how she'd felt yesterday when Jackson had asked her if she wanted to kiss him again.

Especially because she'd wanted to kiss him something awful, to experience that dizzy feeling of his lips moving over her own. She'd also wanted more. To pull back the lapels of that pristine white shirt and bare his gorgeous chest to her eyes and her lips and her hands.

She'd wanted him joined to her, moving in her, loving her.

The thought crashed in and Helena nearly dropped the crystal serving bowl she'd been carrying to the table.

"Stop that right now," she whispered. "Don't think. Just—just cook. That's all he ever asked you to do. Well, mostly all he ever asked you to do. It's all he wants at least, so just work.''

That was best—and all there was time for, anyway. There was this party and then Oliver's celebration. She hoped Jackson's plans stayed on schedule, because her time was coming. She could feel it. The changes in her body were becoming more pressing. There'd been those little twinges low in her back yesterday and the day before. The ones that had started and then gone away.

She wanted her time to be here, for her child to arrive, but she wanted to help Jackson finish what they'd started, too.

When they had done that, it would be just her and her child. That was the way she wanted things, wasn't it?

The question still chased her hours later. The doorbell was ringing over and over. Jackson was dressed in black and white. He was looking incredibly cool, smiling as he greeted his guests, and Helena was hoping she didn't look too cumbersome in her pink dress as she placed the last of the hors d'oeuvres on the serving cart and moved everything into the dining area.

"Leave that, Helena. I'll see to it," Jackson was saying, taking the plate she was lifting. "Come visit with your friends. They're all eager to see you and make sure that you're feeling all right. Here, I've made a place for you."

He led her to the plushest, most comfortable chair in the living room.

She looked up at him to protest, and he placed one finger over her lips. He fussed with the collar of her dress and smoothed back a long strand of her hair that was trying to slide over her eye.

"Sit. Please," he whispered, and she could deny him nothing. She sat.

Looking around, Helena was astounded at the number of people gathered here. She'd helped issue the invitations herself, so she wasn't surprised to see Eric, Sharon Leggit, Hugh and Marie Brannigan, or John Nesbith. But in addition there were several local children and their parents whom she'd spoken to on the street, children whose talent she had mentioned to Jackson. There was Ellen Hilson who saved the dogs, and June Sorenson, who at age sixty had decided to finally get her college degree after the death of her husband. Betty Rice, who helped keep Main Street looking pretty by adding flowers from her own garden to the ones the city supplied, was seated on a couch. Elliott Woodford was there, although Helena wasn't quite sure why. Abe, too. And Alma. Obviously Jackson had issued some invitations she hadn't been aware of.

"They're your friends, Helena," he whispered, low enough so no one nearby could hear. "And your family," he added, glancing toward the door to where Eric was indeed admitting her family, and she looked up in consternation.

"This party was so you could mingle with the people you were considering for your benefit," she said, shaking her head.

"Originally," he conceded, "but—Lilah and I had a little talk a few days ago. We decided to make a few minor changes."

"What if I don't have enough food?"

Jackson chuckled. "Umm, you've been cooking all day, Helena."

"Yes, but—"

"And Lilah's bringing a cake. Alma brought a few things, too. Everything will be fine."

Jackson was looking very pleased with himself. Helena was feeling terribly confused.

At that moment Alma calmly reached into the huge tote bag she carried everywhere with her, pulled out a piece of folded-up cloth, walked over and handed it to Jackson.

He disappeared into the kitchen, returning with a hammer and nails. Nodding to Bill, Jackson unfolded the cloth and the two of them hung it over the archway joining the dining room to the living room.

Best Wishes To Helena And Baby Austin, the banner read.

"Surprise!" everyone called, and packages appeared from behind backs.

Helena slid one hand up over her mouth. She stared directly into Jackson's eyes.

"You were spending so much time on my concerns, I thought perhaps you hadn't had time to take care of all the things you needed to," he confessed. "Besides, it was simply a good excuse for all the people who care about you to have a chance to show you how much you matter."

His voice was low and warm as he took her hand and touched his lips to her palm. Heat arced through her body. She folded her fingers closed over the place where Jackson's lips had been.

"I—thank you," she said as he stepped back and let her friends crowd in close. She could feel him drawing farther and farther away. He'd set this in motion, but now he was bowing out. She knew why. This party was about the baby.

Jackson had reason to feel uncomfortable dealing with thoughts of babies. He'd been betrayed by the two women he'd cared about and should have been able to count on the most in the world. He'd thought he was being given the gift of a child and it had been snatched from him. No matter what he said, she knew those issues weren't behind him, just as she knew he wasn't going to place his trust in another woman's hands again. He wasn't going to have a child of his own, ever.

But he would honor hers in this way.

As Helena opened packages of baby blankets, bibs and tiny white shirts a doll could wear, she looked over the heads of the loving group surrounding her. "Thank you. Thank you all," she said, but her gaze was directed at Jackson.

He smiled sadly and saluted her. "Be happy," he mouthed.

She would try. She really would try for his sake and the sake of her child.

But at that moment, as she sat surrounded by wrapping paper and baby toys, the doorbell rang again. Alma volunteered to get it. When she returned, she was dragging Barrett behind her.

"I heard there were festivities," he said, looking terribly sophisticated and out of place in the midst of all the baby items. Of course, there was no way Helena would ever believe that Jackson had invited the man. Once again, he was interloping on Jackson's territory. He had walked away with Jackson's wife, lain with the woman who had pledged to be Jackson's for life, planted a child where Jackson's child should have grown. Now here he was again, looking not the least bit ashamed.

"No festivities here, I'm afraid," Helena said, without so much as a trace of guilt. "Just a group of close friends." She stared at him pointedly.

He didn't even bother to look guilty. Instead he moved closer to her. "I brought you something, something I think you'll like," he said, lowering his tone to that of a lover.

When he held out a package wreathed in pink-and-blue baby shower paper, Helena knew that word of the party had leaked out. It had been Alma's doing, no doubt, but she couldn't really be mad at her friend. Alma's transgressions were usually made when she was excited about something that she considered wonderful. She didn't gossip out of spite.

Helena looked at the package.

She frowned at the man. "You should be ashamed of yourself. What kind of person are you?" she reprimanded. "Don't you have any sense of right and wrong at all? Didn't anyone ever teach you how to behave?"

In the back of her mind Helena realized that none of her friends would realize what she was talking about. They didn't know about Jackson's wife. "You should have…called," she finished lamely.

For just a second she thought she saw Jackson smiling, but of course, that couldn't be. Not when this man he disliked so much had invaded his home.

"You should have definitely called," she said more firmly. "And you—" She stood suddenly, bits of wrapping paper and ribbon sliding off her lap. Anger at the hurt he had inflicted on Jackson, at the fact that he was still trying to hurt him, surged through her.

"You should apologize to Jackson, Mr. Richards. You should beg his forgiveness."

A startled look came over Barrett's face, even a slight flush, and then a frown. A stubborn frown, exactly the kind that a little boy would wear if he'd been caught misbehaving and was too stubborn to admit his guilt. The package hung in his hand like an enormous weight he didn't know how to release.

Helena almost wanted to feel sorry for him. Every bad man had once been a baby as full of promise as her own child. Something terrible had happened to make that child turn into this self-centered creature. She couldn't help regretting that, but the thought of what he'd done to Jackson wouldn't allow her to defuse the situation.

She looked up across the room into Jackson's eyes. He stared at her, he smiled at her, then he looked around the room at the other startled guests. He glanced at the package that Barrett still held.

Crossing the room, Jackson came to her. "It's all right," he said gently. "Your friends are...curious, Helena. Why don't you open the package and let them see what's inside?"

She thought she understood. Her friends had come to have a celebration for her. They didn't know about Barrett's background. Jackson had planned this party for her and her baby. He wanted it to be a happy occasion, even if he had to be polite to a man who had wronged him.

Helena nodded. She took the package out of Barrett's hands and removed the paper. Inside was a set of gold-plated baby dishes.

"Beauty for the child of a beauty," Barrett said, stumbling a bit over his words as he tried to reclaim his poise. He started to take her hand. She quickly moved to pick up the wrapping paper, busying herself so that her hand was unavailable.

Was that laughter she saw in Jackson's eyes?

"I hope you'll remember me when you use this," Barrett said, and suddenly she didn't know whether to laugh—or to cry. How could Jackson's wife have chosen this phony man over the reality of her husband?

But Helena knew.

Her husband hadn't loved her. She'd probably longed for him to do so, had been lost knowing that he never would. She'd turned to someone else instead.

Wouldn't any woman?

No.

The word echoed through Helena's mind. A woman who truly loved Jackson wouldn't settle for any other. She would never turn from a man of Jackson's integrity to a man who had none.

"Do you like it, my dear?" Barrett was saying, and there was definitely a slight air of little-boy anxiety in his words. "What did Jackson give you?"

She remembered that Oliver had treasured Jackson, but he had not cared for Barrett. She wondered what it would be like to go through life trying to best a man like Jackson, trying to be even half as good as him, to live in his shadow, knowing you could never be quite good enough.

That didn't excuse Barrett's behavior.

She stared into Jackson's eyes and she smiled. "Jackson gave me this day," she said softly. "He planned all this, but your gift is very nice," she added politely, speaking not to the man she could never like but to the deprived child this man must once have been.

Hours later, after Jackson had shepherded out the last guest and the last helper he'd hired to clean up, he turned to her.

"You handled that situation with Barrett very tactfully, Ms. Austin," he said, placing his hands on her shoulders and kneading slightly.

"Umm," she said, lolling her head to one side. "I—well, I confess that I began to be a little sorry for him after I got over being angry. What must it be like for him to have spent so many years trying to be you and knowing he'll never succeed?"

"I think you've just complimented me," he said, his voice low and husky and seductive as he slid his gifted fingers up beneath her hair, lightly massaging her scalp.

"Oh, yes," she agreed, to both his comment and his touch. "You don't have any idea how much people look up to you, do you?"

"Why don't you tell me while I take care of you?" He touched his lips to the crown of her hair.

Her voice seemed to disappear into the ether somewhere. She struggled to find it. "Well," she finally managed to say, the sound coming out somewhat choked and broken. "Well, people—people respect you. They know you're a man in charge. They know that you're honest, that you care about them and about justice. You can't be bought, and you don't say things you don't mean. Barrett's not like that. He's just a pretend version of you, an imperfect knockoff. I suspect that he knows it, too. Don't you think it's sad that he'll never be what he wants to be?" Her voice was drifting. Jackson's body seemed closer, warmer, inviting her to lean into him.

"Don't you…think so?" she said again.

"Umm, you're talking about my archenemy here," he said lazily, but Helena noted the humor in his voice and that he kept tracing lazy circles on her scalp with his fingertips. It was deliciously decadent. She leaned her head back into his hands.

"You don't have anything to fear from him."

"I have evidence to the contrary. My wife thought differently."

Helena stood silent for a moment, not sure how to phrase her thoughts. Then she lifted her head and looked into Jackson's eyes. "I—I hope you won't be offended if I say this, but I think—no, I'm pretty sure that your wife was somewhat foolish. If I had been in her place, I would have—"

Jackson's fingers stilled. He slid his hands down to cup her shoulders and he pulled her closer. "What would you have done, Helena, if you had been my wife?"

His words came out on a fierce whisper. They caught at Helena's heart, and she couldn't answer.

She would never be his wife. She would never be his love.

Slowly she shook her head. "It doesn't matter. I'm not going to be your wife, and it's probably unfair to the woman who held that position to speculate on what I would have done if I were in her shoes. Let's—let's forget it. I should get home."

She rubbed at the small of her back.

"Helena?" There was tension in Jackson's voice. He placed his large hand where her small one had massaged her back.

She gasped slightly.

"What is it?"

"I'm not sure. My back is aching. It's done that several times in the last few days. False labor. The only thing is, this time it's not stopping."

"And that would mean...what?" He framed her face with his hands and forced her to look into his eyes.

"I think...I think it means it's time for me to go to the hospital."

"Then we'll go. I'll call Lilah," he told her.

Helena shook her head. "She had to go to Portland on business right after the party. She won't be back until tomorrow afternoon. The baby wasn't due for a few more weeks."

He looked down at her, his eyes dark and filled with sudden concern. "Then we'll go without Lilah."

Helena tried to smile. "I suppose there've been lots of women who've gone into labor without a coach."

"But not you," he promised. "I don't know anything about coaching a baby into the world, but I won't leave your side. I'll learn what I need to know. You just concentrate on the things you need to concentrate on. Forget everything else. Let me worry about all the rest."

And he wrapped his arm around her shoulders and guided her out the door.

Chapter Ten

Jackson's hands gripped the steering wheel tightly. He was driving too fast, but not nearly fast enough to suit himself.

Helena was having her baby, and he was all she had to rely on right now. The hospital seemed much farther away today than it had the day before.

"Are you all right?" he asked, taking his eyes off the road for just a second to look at her. She tried to smile up at him and nod, but he heard her sudden gasp.

"You're not. You're hurting," he said as he pressed the accelerator farther toward the floor.

"I'm supposed to hurt," she managed to say, but when he turned to look again, her eyes were closed. She was in incredible pain, and all he could do was keep driving. He wanted to hit himself for being so useless to her right now.

What could he do? What helped when a person was in pain? He'd been there a number of times himself.

Not like this, but he'd sustained a few knife wounds when he was younger. His mother had beaten the pulp out of him more than once. He and Barrett had once bloodied each other pretty well. What had he done then? What had worked?

Distraction. That was what Lamaze was about anyway, wasn't it? At least to some extent.

Helena gasped again. A moan escaped her, but he could tell she was trying to choke it back. He wished he'd spoken to Lilah, learned what to do just in case something like this happened. But he hadn't been thinking, he hadn't wanted to think about this moment, damn him.

What could he do for her? *Think, dammit, Castle, think.*

She tried to muffle a groan. His fingers went white-knuckled on the steering wheel.

He searched his mind for some way to distract her from the pain flooding her body.

"Helena," he began, his voice ragged, "do you know…do you know the recipe for—" He struggled for the name of a food and found that his thoughts had scattered to the wind.

"A recipe?" Confusion, maybe even a trace of indignation colored her words. She was panting slightly as the contraction passed. "You want to talk recipes right now?"

No, he didn't, but he didn't know the things that Lilah knew. He didn't know the breathing exercises.

"It might help," he said lamely, "if we could find something to take your mind off some of the pain. I suggested recipes only because it's part of who you are. You create them, you live with them, you might remember one or two."

She tried to laugh and pat his hand, but he could tell that even in this downtime, she was still struggling. Why on earth weren't they at the damn hospital yet?

"Helena, sweetheart?"

"It's okay. I'm okay." But he could tell that she was not.

"Helena?"

He looked at her and she nodded. "Okay," she said on a breath. "Tiramisu."

"First ingredient, angel," he prompted. "Take a breath first. Don't forget to breathe."

"I won't," she gasped out. "First ingredient semisweet chocolate."

"Okay, breathe," he coached. "Next ingredient?"

"Sugar," she said weakly as he pulled up in front of the hospital. He threw the car into Park, climbed out and rushed to the passenger side.

"Egg yolks," she was saying as he lifted her into his arms and drew her close.

As he strode into the emergency room, Helena continued reciting instructions for making the dessert.

"She's having a baby," he said to the receptionist.

"You're her husband?"

"I'm her husband," he lied without hesitation. No way was he letting anyone separate him from Helena tonight. Just let someone try.

At that moment a wheelchair was brought forward. He gently lowered Helena into it and a nurse stepped forward to wheel her away.

Jackson could hear her breathing becoming more labored. The pains were starting again. He turned to the woman waiting for him to fill out the financial paperwork.

He tossed her his credit card. "I'm going with her. Forget the details of the insurance. I'll take care of whatever needs taking care of. Just give me the paperwork to sign so that I can be gone."

"I don't know when you last stayed in a hospital, Mr....Castle," the woman said, looking at his card, "but it can be quite expensive. I don't think you understand."

He thinned his lips, stared directly into the woman's eyes. "I assure you I'm more than capable of covering the tab. I'm also more than willing. What's more, I'm going now. My wife needs me. If you want me to sign anything, now's the time. Otherwise, hit me with it later."

For two seconds she hesitated. Then she pushed a paper in front of him. Jackson signed it without reading it.

"Where?" he demanded.

"Second floor. They'll be prepping her. Then you can be with her."

Fifteen minutes later he found himself in a birthing room with Helena.

"I suppose I should have called one of my brothers," she said from her position in a rocking chair. "I still could."

He shook his head. "The nurse told me that your contractions are pretty close together for a first birth. I'm here and I'm staying."

"I'm sorry," she said.

"Don't be. I want to be here. I want to help." He stared into her sweet aqua eyes and he could see when the distressing pain began to surface, even before she gritted her teeth.

He reached out and grasped her hands. "Let me

help. Look in my eyes. Talk to me, Helena. Lean on me.''

She talked to him. She told him how she was supposed to breathe and he did his best to coach her through.

When the pain got too bad, he rubbed her back. When her hair became damp and clung to her cheeks, he called for ice chips and fed them to her.

Through hours of labor he strove to take her pain, wished he could actually do so.

Damn, but he felt inadequate to the task. The pains were getting worse, much closer together.

''I need to push,'' she insisted, her voice breathy and frantic.

''Not quite yet,'' the doctor told her. He looked at Jackson.

Jackson nodded and turned to Helena. ''Let's talk about something else. Did I ever tell you about the time Oliver was called to school because I was caught looking up a girl's dress?'' he asked.

A long hiss issued from between Helena's teeth. ''Do you think I—care? Do you think—do you think I want to—know about that?''

Jackson almost wanted to smile, but he didn't. Her out-of-character response told him just how much pain she was in.

''I'll tell you a little of it anyway,'' he said, desperately hoping that if he distracted her, annoyed her enough, she wouldn't feel the pain. He launched into a story that had only the most rudimentary basis in fact, not much to do with the actual incident from his childhood, the whole thing designed to steal Helena's attention from her urge to push.

''Of course, Eleanor wasn't a real woman. She was

this mannequin they kept in the life sciences room, but at fourteen in an all-male school she was just about the closest thing I was going to get to a full-blooded woman at the time. The lady had absolutely nothing on you, though, angel. Those synthetic legs couldn't even begin to compare to the sweet soft curves of yours. You ready for another story, darlin'?''

"I'm—I'm not ready for anything. I'm going to pay you back for this, Jackson," Helena threatened breathlessly.

The doctor gave Jackson a sympathetic smile. "All the mothers say that to the fathers. Of course, this is different. You're—"

Of course the doctor knew Jackson wasn't the father. He knew Helena. Jackson said a silent prayer of thanks to the man for not kicking him out of the room.

Just then Helena gave a long, low moan. "Please," she begged. "Please, now."

Her plea was so plaintive, so filled with anguish, Jackson couldn't help turning to the doctor. "Doctor?"

The man nodded. "Yes, now. She can push. You can help her. Count to ten between pushes. Help support her."

Jackson wrapped his arm around Helena's back as the doctor and nurse eased her into position. "Push, angel," he said, but she already was.

"Now count. One-two-three..."

"Four-five-six..." she said with him. "Please, now."

"Not yet. Nine-ten," he said, moving forward to where the count should be. "Now."

Together they counted. They pushed. Over and

over again. She grew agitated, her moans grew louder, her breathing more labored.

"I—I—I can't count anymore," she said.

"Push one more time," the doctor urged. "Big push." And Helena clamped down on Jackson's fingers so hard that her skin seemed to fuse to his. He strove to give her as much of his strength as he could.

"Here it comes," the doctor warned, and Helena bore down again.

With a grunt and a slight cry, Helena pushed her child out into the world right into the doctor's hands.

The big man smiled as Helena panted, trying to catch her breath. "She's here. You did it, Helena. She's here at last."

For several seconds Helena seemed not to react to the news. Then she slumped back against Jackson. "She's here, Jackson. I have a daughter," she said breathlessly, her sweet, battered body resting against his.

Jackson smiled down at her. He urged her against his shoulder. He stroked his palm over her damp hair. She smiled up at him, then looked toward the tiny bit of humanity the doctor was holding.

"Would you like to cut the cord?" the man asked Jackson, and Jackson was surprised to find that his hands were shaking as he took the scissors.

He was awed by the sight of the helpless little bundle, the baby girl the nurse finally placed in Helena's arms. He was humbled by the vision of the baby rosebud lips seeking out her first meal against Helena's creamy skin. A cathedral couldn't have been more silent, more awesome than the sight of new life entering the world and taking her place.

For long seconds Jackson simply watched. For several seconds more, he tried to talk himself into standing.

A sense of being cheated came over him. He wasn't needed here anymore. He'd done what he was here for. He no longer had a purpose here.

Slowly he rose to his feet and looked down at Helena and her baby.

"Isn't she wonderful?" she asked, gazing at her child.

"She's perfect," he agreed, trailing his hand down Helena's cheek as he leaned to kiss her forehead. "I'll leave you to get acquainted with your daughter now."

He turned to the door.

"Jackson?" Helena's voice was soft and uncertain. He looked over his shoulder at the picture she and her child made. Sweetness and innocence personified.

"Stay," she said softly. "Just for a few minutes. You could rest here," she said, indicating the rocking chair she'd occupied earlier. "You must be tired."

He was anything but tired. He was energized, restless, exhilarated, frustrated. But he sat, he stayed, he watched the most beautiful scene he'd ever seen. And he knew that he'd remember this moment forever, long after he and Helena had said their last goodbyes.

Her emotions were on a wild roller coaster, all hills and valleys, Helena thought two days later as she and her child left the hospital on her brother Bill's arm.

For two days she'd spent her time getting acquainted with her baby, Beth Ann, and that had been wonderful, joyous, enlightening.

For two days she'd realized that her life had changed and that Jackson was moving out of her sphere, getting ready to leave her and Beth behind.

And that had been…hellish, a mix of being glad she'd had the chance to know him and a frantic, foolish need to beg him not to leave. To beg him to love her enough to trust her and stay with her.

"But he's not gone yet, sweetie," she whispered in her daughter's ear, drawing her child close.

"What?" Bill asked, maneuvering her and Beth Ann through the hospital in the wheelchair they'd insisted she use.

"Nothing," Helena said absently. "I just meant that it was good to be going back home to my life and my routines."

He chuckled. "I suspect those routines will be a little different now."

"Umm, I know, but I won't mind. I like constant activity. I like being useful." And she still had a little more time to fit being useful for Jackson into her life.

"You're absolutely not doing this," Jackson told her when she showed up several hours later with Beth Ann in her baby basket. "You've only just come home from the hospital."

She wrinkled her nose at him. "I had a natural birth. No surgery to recover from, no dangers to overcome. I'm a little sore and a little tired, but that just means I'll take more frequent rests, and as you can see, Bethie is just going to snooze when she wants to. In the meantime, when she's sleeping, I can do a thing or two for you."

"There's not much left to be done. You worked hard these past few weeks. You prepared everything."

"Exactly. That's why I'll be able to take care of the little that needs taking care of."

"I don't want you to." Jackson's voice was sterner than she'd ever heard it, his expression more grim, and finally Helena got it.

"You don't want me here?"

"That's not what I said."

But it was what he meant. She remembered that he'd never really wanted her there in the first place. She reminded him of the woman who had betrayed him, and now that her baby was here, he was probably reminded even more of what he'd lost to Barrett. Of course, that would be difficult for him to live through. And there truly wasn't much left to do, only the final cooking.

"I—I suppose I don't actually have to be here. I've already drawn up the menu for Oliver's tribute. I could do the cooking at my own house this time. All of it will have to be transported into town, anyway," she stammered.

He touched her arm. A touch so brief, so obviously meant only to get her attention, that pain stabbed at her heart. Everything was winding down, the hourglass had almost filled with sand. The tribute was only two days away, and he was trying to be kind, to begin to sever the ties without hurting her. He was also, she remembered, one of the "world's most wealthy bachelors." He would be used to severing ties with women.

"I appreciate you, Helena. I value you and your work," he told her. "But you have other concerns now. Your life has changed. The importance of this tribute pales in comparison to what you have waiting for you now."

She shook her head. "It means a great deal to you."

"I don't want to just be taking from you, dammit, Helena. For once I want to give you something you need. You need this time to rest. Like it or not, I'm importing a few cooks from Boston for the day. You're not doing anything more than calling out instructions."

But she shook her head vehemently. "Don't lie and say you've just taken. You helped me give birth to my child."

"Let me give more. Something you really need right now."

But she knew he could never really give her what she needed from him. She knew in that moment, as she began to lose him, that she didn't want to *ever* lose him.

But she couldn't let him know how much she cared. It just wouldn't be fair when he'd warned her so many times. This wasn't like the other disappointments in her life. She'd always known Jackson would go. He hadn't made her a single promise he was breaking. She tried to regain her composure. "You want to give me time to spend with my baby?" she asked gently.

"I'm insisting on it."

She sighed. "All right. You're the boss, Jackson."

He stared down at her, his eyes dark and fierce. They both knew that he would not be her boss after this tribute. After that he would just be her former employer. Nothing more.

Except in her heart, where he would always be a great deal more.

"I don't want to make you unhappy," he said gently.

She wondered if he knew that she had fallen in love

with him, if he worried about having another woman on his conscience. She didn't want to be a regret to him. And so she smiled.

"I'm not unhappy. Hey, I get to boss around a whole group of big-city chefs. What woman wouldn't like that?" she managed to say.

He smiled back and gently brushed his knuckles across her cheek. "Surely not you. Be happy, Helena," he whispered.

She nodded. "Let's end this right," she agreed.

His smile was sad as he lowered his head and kissed her lips.

"Yes," he said, his warm breath joining with hers. "Yes, let's end this right."

But those words took on a new meaning when Helena got back to her house. The message light on her answering machine was blinking.

"Welcome home, sweet Helena." Barrett's too-smooth voice slid out of the machine when she pressed the button. "I thought you might like to know that my lovely wife is coming to town for the celebration. Perhaps you'd like to meet her. The two of you have so much in common. Jackson...and me. Let's make it a party, shall we? The two of you can compare notes."

Helena knew then that there would be no chance to end things right. Things were going to get complicated.

She was going to have a lot more to do than just call out instructions, because she would be damned before she'd let Jackson be subjected to further humiliation by those two. She was going to make it her personal quest to keep them far away from Jackson,

even if it meant giving up the goodbye she'd hoped
to have with the man she loved. And she had just the
four big brothers to help her.

Helena picked up the phone and began to dial.

Chapter Eleven

The day of Oliver's tribute dawned bright, wind free and darn near perfect weatherwise, so why did he feel so apprehensive? Jackson asked himself when he woke up early that morning.

Maybe because he wasn't just worried about the fate of the tribute. More likely because he was worried about the fate of one woman and her tiny infant. Maybe he *was* a lot more like the Austin brothers than he realized.

He didn't like leaving Helena to her own devices. Now that she had a baby to care for, her life was even more frantic. But did that mean she'd slowed down? Hell, no. What had he expected, when Helena was the kind of woman who'd just naturally see to everyone else before she saw to herself?

Maybe in time she'd link up with Eric. The thought was like a harpoon to the heart, but it had to be considered. Eric was the kind of man who would know just what to do with a good, loving woman and a sweet little baby. Maybe Helena would eventually marry the man.

And maybe she wouldn't.

And maybe none of that was any of his damn business.

Jackson scrubbed his hands back through his hair. He swore beneath his breath. He resigned himself to the way things were and decided that he would be fine with all of this once he had gotten clear of Sloane's Cove and the old sentimental memories this place evoked.

By the time Helena slipped into his room three minutes later carrying a tray of eggs and fruit and freshly baked muffins, he was even able to smile. She was looking so deliciously guilty and pink.

He raised one brow. "Breakfast in bed?" he asked, sitting up and draping the sheet over his hips.

She put the tray down on the nightstand and pushed her hair back with one hand. "I...th-thought you might have a lot on your mind today." To her credit, she stammered only slightly. "Maybe you need more time to plan. It's the big day, after all, but I didn't want you to miss out on a hot breakfast. Today of all days you need a good meal to start the day off right, and besides, you—you overslept."

He hadn't. He'd been in here worrying about her, but she didn't need to know that. Instead he smiled to make her feel less uncomfortable about being in his bedroom. "Where's Bethie?"

"Sleeping in the crib you brought in for her. Well, she *was* sleeping," she said as the tiniest sound of movement issued from the room two doors down.

"She'll be needing you."

Helena nodded. "She's probably almost ready for breakfast herself."

Jackson sucked in a deep breath. His blood still ran hot thinking about Helena holding her baby to her breast. It was such an intimate gesture, such a necessary gesture, life and love brought down to its most basic level. A mother providing nourishment for her child from her own body.

Something dark and hopeless twisted deep inside him.

He ignored it. It didn't matter, anyway. In one more day he'd be back to his life and his business, and he knew full well how that went. His business took up his hours, it consumed his soul. He liked it that way. If he was attracted to a woman, he knew that sooner or later his business would clash with the woman—and the business would win. That had always been his way. These past few weeks had been a brief hiatus, a small voyage into craziness, but now it was over, and that was, no doubt, a good thing, an inevitable thing.

"You'd better go see to Beth," he urged Helena gently. "I'll be up soon."

As she walked away, he took a bite of the food she had brought him. It was no doubt one of the best breakfasts he'd ever eaten…but his attention wasn't on food.

It was on what was happening two doors down.

Jackson was as ready as he'd ever be, he thought as he and Helena drove toward the park with Bethie in the back seat of the car he'd rented to accommodate her carrier. He should be feeling a sense of elation, he thought. He was on the way to accomplish what he'd set out to do. Satisfaction should be burning in his gut. Instead, he felt a sense of dread and loss.

Of course, it was just temporary—it would fade away once he'd left this town. Still, at the moment it felt...real. It was all he could do to keep his eyes on the road and off the woman he was about to leave for the last time.

Suddenly her fingers brushed against his arm. He jerked the wheel, nearly sending them off the blacktop.

"You're sure everything's all right?" Helena asked.

He chose to believe she was talking about the tribute to Oliver.

"I hired an army of high school students. By now they've transported everything, set up the tables and hung the banners. The florist has arranged the flowers, the musicians are tuning up and the champagne is starting to flow. Your sister told me she'd let me know if anything was amiss when she arrived, and my cell phone hasn't rung."

"I just want everything to be perfect for you."

He glanced down at Helena, delicate and lovely in palest yellow. Out of the corner of his eye he could see the tiny form of little Beth, yawning, her little fists waving.

"Everything's perfect," he assured Helena.

And it was. At least physically. When they arrived at the green in the center of town, a string quartet was in the white latticework bandstand playing Pachelbel's Canon. The wealthy visitors who had stormed the town were wolfing down Helena's pâté, chattering away at the beauty of the banks of white roses and baskets of purple and gold pansies that enhanced the greenery of the already lovely park. Sailboats could be seen rocking in the harbor just a half block away. An artist couldn't have painted a prettier setting.

This was what he had come for. This was the day he had planned and looked forward to. This was also a day of goodbyes, both to Oliver and to Helena.

Jackson felt a terrible urge to pick Helena up in his arms and carry her away from here, to put off the inevitable end. Instead, he smiled down at her.

"Ready?"

Helena nodded up at Jackson. She felt herself getting lost in the intensity of his silver-gray gaze, but that wouldn't do. She had to stay alert and on guard.

It had been two days since that call from Barrett, but she had no doubt that he'd be here today.

So when Jackson smiled down at her and offered her his arm to lead her to the risers and podium that had been set up next to the bandstand, she shook her head.

"Good luck," she whispered.

He leaned forward, grinning down into her upturned face. "You think I'm doing this alone, then, do you?"

"Of course. It's your day."

"Angel, it's Oliver's day. A day to honor him and the people who will benefit from his having existed and having been the man he was. At least, that's what I want it to be. No way do I plan to leave you down here when you spent so much time on this project. Now, come on. Hand little Beth Ann over to one of your siblings and come with me, love."

He held out his hand in invitation.

She looked up into his eyes. She wanted nothing

more than to stand beside him, to show him her support, to just be next to him for as long as she could. But she might be needed down here.

"Bethie might need me," she said, knowing those were the magic words.

His face turned solemn. "You're right," he said, brushing her cheek with his finger. "Here goes." And he moved up the steps, his long strides carrying him to the podium.

He had never looked more elegant or imposing or handsome...or unattainable, Helena thought. It was the last such thought she would allow herself. She hugged her daughter close and, under the pretext of digging into her diaper bag, avoided the obvious seated area and moved to the edge of the crowd.

She could hear Jackson clearly from there, but she could also see everyone else. If Barrett arrived and tried to do something, she would be ready. She scanned the crowd one more time, then turned her attention to Jackson.

He was staring straight at her. He was giving her that lazy, knowing smile that she'd grown to dream of at night. She clutched that feeling to her. After today, feelings and dreams and memories were all she'd have. But for today, she also had his presence, his voice that could soothe or command...or seduce.

"Thank you for having me here," he said to the crowd in that wonderful voice. "When I came here three weeks ago, I didn't know any of you who live here in Sloane's Cove. All I knew of this town was the memory of a man who saved my life one day many years ago. Oliver Davis was a good man. He looked beyond the obvious flaws of a human life and demanded better. There are a number of people in this audience who were given lifesaving opportunities thanks to Oliver. Like me, they've come here because he made a difference to them.''

Helena wanted nothing more than to watch Jackson and Jackson alone, but she couldn't do that yet. Indeed, when she glanced away from the podium to the side where the entrance to the park lay, she saw that a car had just pulled up. A beautiful dark-haired woman was getting out. She carried a dark-haired child of about three. A man was coming around the car, but he wasn't looking at the woman or the child. His eyes were scanning the crowd. A frown marred his too-pretty face.

Quickly Helena turned to look back up at Jackson and found him studying her quizzically.

She managed to smile.

''I suspect Oliver thought his work would be done when he died, but we're here today to make sure that his legacy lives on,'' Jackson continued. ''I've come here to honor his memory, and I've had some very special help along the way. I'm sure you all know Helena. She's one very special lady.''

His voice dropped low and deep. He smiled again then, and the crowd turned to look her way.

''I came here looking for three good people to carry on what Oliver had started,'' Jackson said. ''I asked Helena to help me. Today it pleases me to announce the recipients of the Oliver Davis Memorial Fund.'' He turned his attention back to the waiting crowd.

A delighted murmur drifted through the crowd, followed by enthusiastic applause. Helena thought she heard a disgusted curse from Barrett, but that was probably her imagination. He couldn't have made his way from the distant entrance to the center of the crowd this fast. But he was moving closer. She knew why he had come. He'd brought his wife and child here to spoil Jackson's day, to humiliate him, to make him remember things that were painful. In truth, Barrett didn't even have to do anything. Just exhibiting the woman and child would be enough. He wanted to be in Jackson's face, to remind him that he'd taken what should have been Jackson's, and he wanted to do it in a very public way, to steal Jackson's and Oliver's thunder.

If he failed to achieve his goal today, he'd try again another day. Helena had no doubt of that. But he wouldn't win today. Absolutely not.

With the crowd still applauding, she raised her fingers to her mouth and blew out a shrill whistle. When Jackson turned surprised eyes her way, she simply smiled back.

That whistle had stood her in good stead as a rough-and-tumble tomboy with four brothers. Now it served as a signal. Out of the corner of her eye she saw her four brothers begin to move toward the edge of the crowd.

She gave Hank a misty-eyed smile as he passed her way.

"Don't worry, babe," he told her. "After what you told me about Barrett the other day, Jackson has our complete sympathy. We won't let anyone wreck the presentation. Bill's about to take a tremendous interest in purchasing some of old Barrett's more... interesting products. We'll keep him occupied for a few minutes, at least."

"For a big brother, you're pretty special," she told him, and rose on her toes to give him a kiss on the cheek. She turned her attention back to Jackson...and discovered that he was looking at Hank. Jackson was wondering what was going on. In another second he would let his eyes wander back over to where her brothers were headed.

She began to walk toward the stage and prayed he'd look her way.

He did. Immediately, as if he'd placed sensors on her, Jackson turned her way. He gave her a dark-eyed, speculative look.

"Changed your mind about joining me, love?" he asked as she neared the stage.

His words nearly broke her heart. She'd love to join him...forever, but for the moment, now that the threat of Barrett was temporarily over, she just wanted to be near Jackson.

Moving up the stairs, Bethie still cradled in one arm, she slid in close to Jackson. He took her hand, twined his long fingers about hers and for a second her heart shifted into overdrive.

"I'm glad you're here," he whispered, leaning away from the mike.

She was glad, too. Standing at Jackson's side felt horribly right. She meant to savor it for the few minutes she had remaining.

He smiled contentedly and turned back to the crowd. "I came here looking for three good people I could help," he said. "I asked Helena to help me, but what she showed me, the people she introduced me to, made me realize that it's impossible to choose the three best or the three most deserving individuals. What I encountered here in Sloane's Cove was an entire community of people who look out for each other. And so, to begin with, the following scholar-

ships will be given out this year.'' Jackson read a long
list that began with Sharon Leggit and John Nesbith.

"Jackson,'' Helena whispered, her voice catching,
"I hope you know how wonderful you are.''

She felt him jerk beside her. He cleared his throat.
She listened as he announced that the scholarships
would be given out annually, that he had also set up
a fund to help local humanitarians, such as Hugh and
Marie Brannigan, and that a third fund would benefit
local artisans and businesspeople. This year's recipi-
ent would be Eric Ryan.

He gazed down into her eyes, his own dark and
fierce. She knew what he was doing. He was setting
up a husband for her because he wouldn't be here to
do the job himself.

Helena felt her throat closing up.

She rose on her toes and kissed him on the cheek
in front of the wildly applauding crowd.

"Let's go,'' he said, his voice a deep growl.

"But your tribute—''

"The most important part is finished,'' he said, and
he turned back to the mike. "In memory of Oliver.
Thank you,'' he said to the photo of the man set up
next to the podium. "You'll never be forgotten.''

"Way to go, Jackson,'' someone called.

"Thank you, Mr. Castle,'' someone else said. "We
won't forget him—or you, either.''

"We won't forget,'' Helena whispered at his side.
"I promise.''

Jackson didn't know if she meant Oliver or himself.
He knew her well enough to know she wouldn't let
Oliver's memory die; he was just foolish enough to
hope she'd remember a man named Jackson, too. But
he cared for her enough and knew himself well

enough, he realized, to know that it would be best for her if she didn't dwell on his own memory for too long.

He took a deep breath. He turned back to the crowd.

"Thank you all for coming today," he said. "I have to fly back to Boston today, but I hope you'll all stick around for the food and the games and the historical displays regarding Sloane's Cove that have been set up around the park. Please, enjoy the day and celebrate in Oliver's memory," he finished.

And in the midst of the ensuing applause, he led Helena down the stairs. She found Lilah and asked her to watch Bethie.

"This way," he urged her, and he led her back among the trees. He walked until the crowd had faded away. Then he turned to her and cupped her jaw with his hand.

"It would have been okay," he told her gently. "I'd already seen Barrett and Denise. But...thank you." He brushed her cheek with his lips. "For caring."

Her eyes widened. She bit her lip. "I'd hoped you wouldn't notice them. If I'd handled this better you wouldn't have, and I could have spared you that much. I'm sorry."

But he smiled. "I'm not. I never would have known you could whistle otherwise," he teased. "You never cease to amaze me, love. So don't be sorry. Be happy. I want you to please be happy."

She nodded slowly, looking up at him with those wide, wonderful blue-green eyes that were slowly misting over. He didn't think he could bear to drag out this goodbye.

"I've arranged for Lilah to drive you and Bethie home," he told her. Because if he drove her home, he'd want to come inside and say goodbye properly. He'd want to do more than just say goodbye.

That couldn't be, for many reasons. She had just had a baby. Her body wouldn't welcome the invasion of a man, but even if that hadn't been so, he didn't want to leave her that way, to make love to her and then walk away. He didn't want to be like the other men who had taken from her and then left her with nothing. And nothing was all he had to offer.

"Your car's all packed, then?" Her voice was small and very un-Helena-like.

"And waiting," he agreed, hoping he could keep his own voice strong and not do or say something they'd both regret.

As it was, he looked down at her and did something regrettable anyway. He touched the silk of her hair. How could he not touch her when she was looking so lost, so much like a woman in need of gentleness?

"You're one special lady, angel," he told her. But she didn't answer him with the smile he'd expected. He supposed other men had told her the same.

And will again, he reminded himself.

"Before you leave, I want to tell you," she said, her voice breaking a bit. "What you did back there, I'll never forget it. You changed lives, Jackson."

But it was only her life he cared about right now. "You've changed *me*," he told her. "You've restored my faith in pregnant women," he said, trying to tease, even though his words were nothing less than the truth.

Finally he had his smile, even if it was a weak, misty one. "I'm glad," she said. "Maybe the next time you meet a pregnant woman who wants to work for you, you'll argue a bit less."

Or remember what he'd left behind, more likely.

"Goodbye, sweetheart," he said, lowering his lips to hers. "Don't let anyone push you where you don't want to go."

"I won't," she whispered fiercely as she rose on her toes and kissed him back, her slender body molding against his own. "Remember this summer."

As if he could ever forget.

He slipped his palms down her back, lifted her against him and drank deeply from her lips. He pressed her to him as if to imprint the memory of her body on his mind forever. He grazed her lips again and again until his need for her was near the breaking point.

"I'll remember," he promised. "Take extra good care of yourself and your baby. Please," he begged.

And then he set her back on the ground, smoothed her hair back from her face, took one last look at the most beautiful woman God had ever made.

He left. Before he could make the mistake of not leaving.

Of begging Helena to give what she'd told him repeatedly she didn't want to give.

Of trying to convince himself that he wasn't the man he'd always been.

Jackson drove off down the road, back to his business, back to his life and his world.

Chapter Twelve

"Well, Bethie, we wanted to make it on our own, and that's what we're doing, isn't it?" Helena asked her child the day after Jackson had gone.

It wasn't even close to the truth. She'd awakened this morning wondering how Jackson was doing, who was taking care of him, how long it would be before he had another woman in his arms and who that woman would be.

Sharp pain had accompanied her thoughts.

"It will go away in time," she whispered to herself as she drove through the town she'd always loved but which felt suddenly empty and lifeless in spite of the fact that the main drag was still as crowded and bustling as ever.

Soon she'd begin forgetting Jackson. She hoped. As it was right now, everything reminded her of him. The people in the town whose lives he'd touched, the streets he'd walked, even her child. Especially the child who'd come into the world safe and sound because of Jackson.

"I'm grateful," she whispered, and she was and would always be. But she also was in love, she forced herself to admit, and that wasn't something she'd wanted. It wasn't what Jackson had bargained for. She'd promised she wouldn't want him.

But she did.

"Well, that's too bad," she told herself and Bethie. "That's not fair at all to Jackson. We'll—we'll just have to get over him. These things happen."

But that was a lie. A man like Jackson didn't happen to most women, ever. He had been different from any other man she'd known. For everything she'd given him, he had given back. He'd made no demands outside of what he'd hired her for. He'd made no promises he hadn't kept.

It wouldn't be fair to look heartbroken and to let anyone know that she was, in fact, mourning the man. Especially not when she knew it would hurt him to know he'd left her wounded and wanting and lying awake wishing he was beside her.

He deserved better than that. For his sake, she'd go on as if things hadn't changed.

And so she wandered into town and met Alma coming toward her with a bag of fruit.

"I don't know what happened today. We've just got too much," the woman told her. "Wish you'd take it. It's probably good for a nursing mother to get all her fruits and vegetables."

Helena blinked.

"Alma?" she asked. She and Alma had been friends forever. They'd shared many things. Alma had tossed her an apple or two now and then at the end of the day when they'd stood chatting. But her friend had never pushed a whole bag of produce at her, at least not in the name of good nutrition. Besides, the day was just beginning. Customers were still pouring in. There was still plenty of time to sell today's stock.

Helena opened her mouth to ask Alma what was going on.

Alma crossed her arms. "For once, don't argue, Helena. Please."

Helena blinked again. Alma wasn't prone to saying please. Something was very wrong here. And the look in Alma's eyes was unreadable. This from a woman who shouted her opinions from the doorway of the fruit stand every day.

"Th-thank you," Helena stammered. "Are you sure you're feeling okay, Alma?"

"Never better. You just make sure you're eating properly. Go on over to the bakery. I hear they've got some great health nut bread. Lots of fiber, lots of vitamins and minerals baked into it. You should try it. Just the thing you need."

Her friend gave her a worried frown. Helena wondered if Alma knew about her broken heart and was trying to mother her past it. But then, Alma had stood by her through other difficult times. She'd never acted this way before.

Helena took the fruit, and the bread that the baker pushed at her. She went home. Her brothers and Lilah stopped by twice that day. Elliott Woodford stopped by once, too. Just to say hello, they all said. Helena wondered if that were true.

She tried to sleep. Between Bethie's need to be fed and her own restless dreams of Jackson, she failed. She kissed her baby and put her back to bed. She closed her eyes and a vision of Jackson appeared before her.

Helena reached out to touch it, but her hand slipped through the vision. She awoke to find herself alone.

"Dammit, Austin," she said as tears slid down her cheeks. "You shouldn't have allowed yourself to fall in love. You knew he was special, that he was different, that he would be the one to finally succeed where no man had really succeeded before, in holding your heart hostage."

She'd known, and she'd been helpless to stop herself. After endless hours, Helena slept, only to have to rise one hour later to feed her child.

"It's okay, sweetie," she crooned, and she tried to convince Bethie and herself that they were better off on their own as they'd planned.

The next morning her doorbell rang. Zeke Delman, a builder, was standing on her doorstep.

"Hi, Helena," he said with a smile. "Remember that soup you made for my wife when she was sick last winter?"

Helena blinked and tried to shove aside her misery. "I...suppose so. I believe it was barley vegetable. Does Linda want the recipe?"

"Hmm? Oh, sure, yeah, I'm sure she does, but really, that's not it. She just really liked it. Really liked it. It was a good thing to do considering how miserable she felt. And you stayed with her for an hour while she ate it and got herself comfortable. So we just wanted to do something for you, too. Thought I'd drop by. You could use a little more room now that you have a little one. Maybe an addition. I've got the plans drawn up right here. Finished them this morning."

"Excuse me?"

"An addition," Zeke said, blushing mightily. "For you and the baby. A playroom. Yeah, that'd be right. See, look?"

She glanced at what appeared to be the blueprints for an addition to her home. "Zeke, I don't think..."

"Yeah, don't. Best if you don't. No charge, of course. On account of the soup. And other things you've done over the years. We just want you to have what you need. You look these over and make sure there's nothing you want changed. If not, we'll go to work getting this beauty up right away. Already talked to the city. Permits here won't be a problem."

When Zeke had left, Helena sank into a chair.

"What's going on?" she asked the walls.

The walls didn't answer, but that day Sharon Leggit and the Brannigans stopped by to make sure she was taking care of herself. Her brothers and Lilah stopped by, too. Alma brought more fruit and bread and fresh milk.

Helena fell asleep on the couch that night. It seemed less big and lonely than her bed, even though she'd been sleeping in the same bed for years.

"Hello, angel," Jackson said in her dreams. "You're all right, aren't you?"

"I miss you," she sobbed.

"Don't," he said gently, reaching out to wipe her tears away. "Don't cry over me. Please."

But there was no stopping her. Her tears woke her.

She swiped them away when Bethie woke, not wanting to convey any undue stress to her baby, but she wondered if Bethie didn't miss him, too. He had held Bethie in his hands right after she'd been born.

He'd smiled at her in awe as if she were the most beautiful thing he'd ever seen.

The night was forever. The only blessing for Helena was that she had her child with her. She talked and sang to Bethie each time the little girl awakened.

As for herself, she didn't go back to sleep. If she slept, she would dream of Jackson, and waking without him would be devastating.

Maybe tomorrow would be better.

But the next day a truck arrived with a full load of diapers and baby clothes. From the Brannigans, the note read, because she was just such a sweet person.

But the Brannigans had given her a gift the very day the baby was born.

That day her brothers and Lilah came by three times. They remarked on the dark circles under her eyes. Eric and John Nesbith stopped in, too. They offered to take care of any chores she needed doing.

Something *was* very wrong here, Helena thought again, sinking down against the wall after the last visitor had left. All these people checking up on her constantly, all these gifts that were all, supposedly, tokens of those who loved her. And the people involved did love her. She had no doubt about that. But she'd known all of them all her life. They showed her their love in small ongoing ways.

These extreme acts of kindness were not what she was used to. Except from one man. One man she ached for so much that she could barely breathe or eat or function.

He was still giving to her in the way he gave to everyone, and she was grateful for his concern.

"But darn it, Bethie, I don't want his gifts. I don't want him to treat me like he treats everyone else."

She'd have to tell him, but she knew that if she spoke to him right now, she'd break down. She'd beg him to love her.

Helena placed the phone beneath a pillow so that she wouldn't be tempted. She lay down and forced herself to lie very still. She forced herself not to think about calling Jackson.

He was dying. Or at least as close to dying as a man could be when there was nothing physically wrong with him, Jackson thought.

It was all because he couldn't see Helena, couldn't be there to assure himself that she was all right. He'd been calling her brothers and her friends, getting reports, and that alone was frustrating. Not nearly enough.

So when the phone rang, he practically jumped on it.

"Jackson?" Lilah said, her voice slightly strained.

"There's a problem," Jackson said, his attention centered squarely on the telephone and nothing else.

"I don't know. She's acting relatively normal. You know, the laugh when you ask her how she is?"

Jackson knew the laugh. He dreamed about her laughing, smiling up at him. He dreamed of lots of things he damn well shouldn't be dreaming about.

He cleared his throat. "I hear a tremendous 'but' in your voice, Lilah," he said.

"She looks...tired. Very tired. And strained, but she won't admit that anything's wrong. I don't think she's getting enough rest and I know darn well something is wrong."

Lilah's diagnosis felt like a ton of lead falling straight through Jackson's body. Something was wrong, and Helena hadn't called. To her, he was just another man who had come and gone. And maybe that was exactly what he was. Just another man.

Dark fear clutched at his insides.

"She's not sleeping?"

"She says it's normal."

He remembered her saying the same thing about her pain when she was in labor. She'd been in agony, but she'd tried to make him feel better.

"Has she seen a doctor?"

"I mentioned her pallor to him, but he says there's nothing physically wrong with her."

She probably snowed the guy just the way she snowed every man alive. With those smiles and that laughter that could melt a man's insides. With that brave front she put on.

"I just thought you'd want to know," Lilah said, "that she's not quite as together as she claims. Oh, and by the way, when I talked to her this morning she mumbled something about you and Zeke Delman and a playroom. She reiterated that she was perfectly fine. Absolutely fine, that she didn't need anyone. And then tears started to slip down her cheeks, even though she did her best to choke them back."

Jackson gasped for air. He swore beneath his breath.

"Jackson?" Lilah choked out the word.

"Tell me."

"Helena never cries. Never. She's always the comforter, the one who pats your back and says, 'there, there.' She never allows herself to be the one on the receiving end. Not even with me. When she finally managed to stop her tears, she apologized profusely and reminded me that she was perfectly fine. I thought you might want to know. I thought you might help. Heck, I even thought you might be responsible. What did you do to her before you left?''

Nothing. Everything, he told himself as he hung up and rubbed his hands over his eyes. He'd kissed her. He'd left her. Now he wasn't there to help her, when anything could have happened to her in the past few days. Maybe she'd just discovered she was in love with Eric and like those idiots before him, he'd used her and left her. Maybe her pigheaded brothers were sending more men to distress her. Jackson didn't know what had brought tears to his angel's eyes, but he knew damn well he was going to find out. Heads would roll, and he wasn't excluding himself from that punishment, either.

He was the jerk who had left her alone when he knew darn well what she was facing. He knew just how tough being a mother was. Hadn't he lived with a woman who'd tried and failed and ultimately given up the job? He'd seen his ex-wife's distress when her new husband had left all the child rearing to her. Knowing that, he'd still walked away from Helena before she'd had time to adjust to her new role in life. He'd known better than anyone how she would struggle to do more than she should. And yet he'd gone, because he was afraid. Afraid of wanting her and having to face the fact that he couldn't have her.

Dark frustration and searing pain tore through him. He wanted to take Helena into himself and protect her. He wanted to hold her. He wanted to…love her. But he realized that he already did.

He swore he'd never force anything on her that she didn't want. He'd never bring her more pain.

But he had to see her again.

As he chartered a plane to Maine and slammed out the door, Jackson realized that for once in his life he wasn't in control of his emotions at all. One small, delicate woman had smiled at him, touched him, and all the protective walls he'd erected his whole life had toppled.

He damn well didn't care.

Helena was having the dream again. Jackson was there before her, close enough to touch, but not real.

She shouldn't bother reaching out. The disappointment was far too crushing when he faded, but...the temptation was too great.

She reached out and her fingertips brushed up against the midmorning shadow of his jaw.

Her eyes flew open. She struggled to sit.

She stared into silver-gray eyes that were...*real.*

Her own eyes flooded with tears.

"Jackson?" Her voice was barely there. So sad and scared. Not like her at all.

"Shh, love. I'm here." And amazingly enough, he sat down beside her on the couch. His weight crushed the edge of the cushion. His hands stroked down her arms, sending delicious curls of sensation through her body.

"How did you get in?"

He chuckled. "Your sister has a key."

Helena frowned. "Traitor."

He frowned back and his breath came sharply. "I'm sorry. You want me to go?"

"No," she said too loudly.

"Good, love, because I'm determined to stay long enough to make sure you're all right."

"And then you'll go?" She tried not to let him know how much that would hurt.

A muscle in his jaw jerked. She touched it with her fingertips. He closed his eyes.

"I'll go," he promised. "Again."

And she would most likely die from the pain this time. At least, it would feel as if she was dying.

"You came because you talked to Lilah," she accused. She'd known Lilah would worry after she'd cried yesterday. She'd tried to stem the flow. "I meant—I meant to let you know I was fine."

"Are you?"

She automatically opened her mouth to say yes, but she couldn't. Tears were building in her throat. When she told him she was fine, when she smiled and laughed and played the part she would have to play, then he would leave. Forever this time.

"Helena? Talk to me, angel."

She tried. She opened her mouth. She closed it again, closed her eyes, tried to keep the tears at bay. Hoping to begin the charade, she nodded.

She took long, deep breaths. She opened her eyes and stared into his. And felt herself drowning completely, except...he looked so worried. She just couldn't allow him to hurt because of her.

"You came because you talked to Lilah. You shouldn't have. I know what she must have told you, but...it's just hormones, I'm sure. I was just being silly."

"Not you. Not ever. And you aren't sleeping, I hear. Is that true?"

She thought about lying. He would worry if he knew just how little sleep she'd been getting.

"I thought so," he said. "Well, we're going to take care of that. We're going to take care of you."

His voice was so seductive she wanted him to go on talking forever.

"How?"

He smiled at her and gathered her into his arms. "Umm, I think we need to set the stage. You're an expert at such things, you know. When you make a meal, it's more than just a meal. It's a production, so I hope you'll be understanding if I'm not as experienced at this as you are, love."

He lifted her high into his arms, against his heart, kissed the top of her head. As he walked past a table on his way back to her bedroom, he picked up a large canvas bag he'd placed there. The pattern on the outside looked familiar. "Alma?" she asked.

He shrugged and looked a bit sheepish. "There wasn't much time. I had a little help."

"Help doing what?"

"Preparing the perfect sleep solution," he said, his breath feathering her hair as the steely strength of his arms surrounded her. Helena thought she could fall asleep if only she could stay here with him forever.

But soon they were at her room. Jackson lowered her to the floor, sliding her down his body. Helena gasped as her skin touched his. She closed her eyes.

"That's right, angel," he said, kissing her eyelids. "Just close your eyes. Sit here for just a minute," he coaxed, leading her to an armchair.

"What—what will you be doing?"

"I'll be preparing your bed."

Helena's heartbeat lost its rhythm for a second. She swallowed hard as Jackson reached into the bag and produced a comforter.

"Feathers," he said. "Very soft and giving, I understand." He smoothed it over the bed, running his hands across the cotton to straighten it. He pulled down the shades.

"Let's take your shoes off," he said, kneeling at her feet and lifting her right foot into his hand. When the shoe slid away, her foot rested in Jackson's large palm. He stroked it along her skin, his nostrils flared and he took a deep breath.

Helena thought she just might faint—or start crying again.

Carefully and quickly Jackson removed her other shoe, then cleared his throat.

"All right, love, onto the bed," he urged, taking her hand and leading her there. "Let's loosen your dress." He said the words dispassionately, but Helena noticed that his fingers trembled as he unfastened the top three buttons at her throat.

"Do you want me to—take it off?" she asked.

He closed his eyes. "Yes, I do," he admitted, "but I don't think that would be wise unless you also wanted me to make love with you."

She did. Above all things, she did. But then she would just be another one of his women. He had not come here for that. He had come here to help her. She knew Jackson. She would let him help her and then he would be on his way.

"I think I can sleep now," she offered, but he only smiled.

"We're not done yet, angel. Lie down, lie back."

She did as she was told and he reached into his bag and pulled out a bottle of lotion. "If you haven't been sleeping, you're probably tense."

She *was*. Incredibly tense. It didn't have a thing to

do with her lack of sleep and had everything to do with the fact that she was alone in a bedroom with the man she loved.

But he wouldn't want to know that.

"Close your eyes, love. We're going to get you to sleep. I'm going to take care of Bethie while you do."

She closed her eyes willingly, hoping to hide the emotion he might read in her eyes.

She heard him picking up the bottle of lotion, opening it, rubbing some of it onto his hands. He slipped his fingers behind her neck and she nearly arched up off the bed. Gently he began to rub slow circles. On her neck, beneath her hair, up into her scalp.

She couldn't help it. She moaned.

"The idea," he said in a choking voice, "is to speak softly, to get you to relax."

She would never relax while Jackson was touching her this way. The tension was rising in her body. It was all she could do not to beg him to touch her other places.

"I came here," he said softly, "because I couldn't deal with the fact that my lovely, lovely Helena wasn't well."

She knew he was just speaking to soothe her, but his words did more than soothe. They nearly broke her heart.

"I'm all right," she tried to tell him, even though it wasn't true. It didn't matter. She would have done anything to keep him from having to hurt, too.

"You're not all right, love," he admonished. "You cried."

His soothing voice broke, and Helena's eyes came open. She reached out and brushed his lips with her fingertips. He closed his eyes and kissed the pads of her fingers.

"You're such a good man," she said. "You were concerned about me. You came here to try to help me." Her voice was barely above a whisper. She couldn't keep the wonder from it as she stared up into this very special man's eyes.

He groaned and leaned closer to her. "Don't make me into a saint, Helena," he said. "I was half-crazy worrying about you and the baby. You do that to me, you know. And I'm here because I just couldn't stay away."

But he should be staying away. He had a business to run, one he'd neglected for weeks. Now here she was, pulling him away from the things he needed to attend to again. He was doing all he could to help her sleep when he had more important things that needed his attention.

"You shouldn't be here," she said abruptly, sitting up so that she was only a breath away from him, so that she was gazing up into his eyes, his chest hard against her softness. "Your business needs you."

"My business can go straight to hell," he said on a moan, sliding his arm behind her back and drawing her close.

And the tears filled Helena's eyes again. Jackson was a businessman, a tremendously successful businessman, and he hadn't become a success by neglecting his work. If he was doing so now, then he truly had gone crazy, or else...

"I'm glad you're here, Jackson," Helena said softly, leaning forward to rest her lips against his own for one brief touch. "Don't worry about me. I'm sorry I dragged you all this way to help me. I—I was just missing you. I guess by now you've guessed that I—I've fallen in love with you.''

He groaned deep in his throat and leaned forward, covering Helena with his body. "I guess I hadn't, but let me tell you, lady, I'm going to treasure that statement. I'm going to ask you to repeat it again. Many times.''

A sliver of alarm ran through her. No doubt tons of women had told Jackson that they loved him.

"I hope you won't let the fact that I love you worry you,'' she whispered. "I know you're not a man who stays or gets involved. It's okay.''

Jackson frowned. "Is it really okay?''

Helena did her best to smile. "It has to be. Living alone was my choice, wasn't it? I told you from the start that you didn't have to worry about me thinking of you as husband material.''

He studied her and swore beneath his breath. "And if I *want* you to think of me as husband material?''

"You don't mean that.''

"I mean that. I want to stay with you, Helena. With you and our baby.''

She breathed in deeply. Her hand slipped over her mouth as her eyes opened wide.

"You mean…another baby.''

"That, too, but I mean Bethie,'' he said firmly. "I delivered her. I held her when she took her first breaths. I placed her at your breast. She's mine. Just let any man say differently.''

His eyes were fierce, but his voice, firm as it was, was uncertain. His fingers trembled on her skin. She loved him for that, for loving Bethie enough to be afraid of losing her. But she wouldn't let him worry about it for very long.

"I won't let anyone say differently," she promised.

"And you, Helena? I love you, you know. I've barely been existing these past few days. Will you stay with me? Will you be mine?"

"Yours and no other man's," she said solemnly. "I *am* yours, Jackson. From the moment I met you, I've been yours."

"Then come be mine, angel." He molded his body and his lips to hers and claimed her for his own.

Helena pressed closer and tasted the pleasure he offered. Then she smiled against his lips. She very nearly laughed with joy.

Jackson smiled back.

"I can't help but notice that you aren't sleeping, love," he told her.

"If I weren't so excited I would be," she said soothingly. "Maybe someday when we've been married for a hundred years, the touch of your hands on my skin will make me want to sleep."

"What does it make you want to do right now, angel?" he coaxed.

"This," she said, slanting her lips over his. "I'm sorry your solution to my problem didn't work, Jackson," she said against his mouth, smoothing her hand over his chest.

He caught it in his own as he drew back to smile down into her eyes.

"Who said it didn't work, love? I have you, don't I? Just where I want you. For the next hundred years, you said?"

"Or maybe more," she promised softly.

"Let's make it more," he said as he covered her mouth with his own.

Epilogue

Six years later, Jackson sat at Bill's birthday party, smiling at the antics of the Austin brothers. He held his two-year-old daughter, Chloe, on his lap. Chloe's twin, Daniel, lay playing at his feet. Bethie was snuggled into the crook of Jackson's other arm.

Helena reached out to take Chloe from him as Jackson stood and whispered to Bethie that there was chocolate cake in the next room and that she had better get some before her uncles stole it all from her.

She giggled up at him, kissed him and scooted away.

He smiled down at his wife, who gazed back at him with loving eyes. He'd never regretted setting up a second office in Sloane's Cove and running most of his business from here, because he loved the town that had brought her into his life.

"You're so beautiful when you're pregnant," he told her.

Helena's eyes opened wide. "How do you know I'm pregnant when I was just going to tell you?"

He shook his head and deepened his smile. "All I have to do is look into your eyes and remember the glow you have when there's life growing within you, love. You do, you know. Glow, that is."

"You don't mind having another after having three in such a short time?" she asked. He had once been a man set on living his life alone, after all. She'd tumbled his plans about something awful.

"You think I regret our children?" he asked, kissing Chloe's cheek. The child cooed as Jackson gave her to the nearest passing uncle, then he hugged Daniel and handed him to one of his aunts. He took his wife by the hand and pulled her close to him, walking toward the door.

"Where are we going?" she whispered conspiratorially.

"Somewhere private," Jackson whispered back, placing his lips near her ear. "Somewhere special. Maybe somewhere where I can put one of those aphrodisiac recipes to use at last. What was it? Something about pine nuts? You never seem to make those, you know."

She laughed up at him. "We never seem to need them, Jackson."

He chuckled. "Hmm, yes, there is that."

"Still," she coaxed, "we're usually not positively rude about finding time to ourselves. We *are* at a party."

"You don't want to be alone?" He stopped and swung her into his embrace.

"Umm," she moaned as his lips teased her jawline. "I'm dying to be alone."

"Good," he said, smiling against her skin. "I'm dying to convince you of how I feel about you. You wondered if I minded having so many babies, if I minded your being pregnant again. As a man who's always believed in actions, love, I thought it was rather important that I show you how much I don't mind. I love you, angel, both when you're slender and when you're growing large with our children," he said, and he stroked his hand over her still-flat abdomen.

She shivered in his arms. Wrapping her arms around him, Helena rose to her toes and placed her lips against his. Soft and then hard. Grazing his lips.

He groaned, deepening the kiss, pulling her even closer.

"This isn't very private," she finally whispered when they had come up for air.

She looked around them and found most of her family's eyes upon them.

Jackson chuckled. "Well, I guess our secret is finally out. We're in love, love," he said.

Helena stroked her hand across his jaw. She turned in his arms. He resettled his arms around her, and their hands rested on her stomach.

"I love you more every year, Jackson," she said. "Thank you for caring for us. All of us." She smiled across the room to where her very large family was gathered.

He chuckled, resting his head on hers. "I wouldn't have it any other way. For a man who once thought he'd live his life alone, I've grown extremely fond of togetherness. I'll show you."

And later that night as he pressed her into the bed and joined his lips to hers, he took his statement a step further. "Being with you, angel, is my greatest gift. Togetherness is wonderful," he whispered as he slid into her body.

She shivered and arched. "Together is heaven," she agreed, twining her arms around his neck.

"Then let's go to heaven, love," he said.

He didn't have to ask twice.

*   *   *   *   *

Helena Austin's twin sister, Lilah,
enlists a sexy billionaire to help
her fend off unwanted suitors
in Myrna Mackenzie's

BLIND-DATE BRIDE.

Look for it in June 2001,
only from Silhouette Romance.

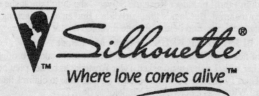

SILHOUETTE *Romance*

COMING NEXT MONTH

#1522 AN OFFICER AND A PRINCESS—Carla Cassidy
Royally Wed: The Stanburys
Military law forbade their relationship, but couldn't stop the feelings Adam Sinclair and Princess Isabel Stanbury secretly harbored. Could they rescue the king, uncover the conspirators—*and* find the happily-ever-after they yearned for?

#1523 HER TYCOON BOSS—Karen Rose Smith
25th Book
Mac Nightwalker was wary of gold-digging women, but struggling single mom Dina Corcoran's money woes touched the cynical tycoon. He offered her a housekeeping job, and Dina quickly turned Mac's house into the home he'd never had. Did the brooding bachelor dare let his Cinderella slip away?

#1524 A CHILD FOR CADE—Patricia Thayer
The Texas Brotherhood
Years earlier, Abby Garson had followed her father's wishes and married another, although her heart belonged to Cade Randell. Now Cade was back in Texas. But Abby had been keeping a *big* secret about the little boy Cade was becoming very attached to....

#1525 THE BABY SEASON—Alice Sharpe
An Older Man
Babies, babies everywhere! A population explosion at Jack Wheeler's ranch didn't thrill producer Roxanne Salyer—she didn't think she was mommy material. But Jack's little girl didn't find anything lacking in Roxanne's charms, and neither did the divorced doctor daddy....

#1526 BLIND-DATE BRIDE—Myrna Mackenzie
Tired of fielding the prospective husbands her matchmaking brothers tossed her way, Lilah Austin asked Tyler Westlake to be her pretend beau. Then Tyler realized that he didn't want anyone to claim Lilah but him! What was a determined bachelor to do...?

#1527 THE LITTLEST WRANGLER—Belinda Barnes
They'd shared a night of passion—and a son James Scott knew nothing about. Until Kelly Matthews showed up with a toddler—the spitting image of his daddy! When the time came for Kelly to return to college, could James convince her he wanted both of them to stay...forever?

RSCNM0501